CUCKOO IN THE NEST

On his deathbed, reclusive million-
aire Sir Harry Trevain asks his
beloved granddaughter, Daisy, to
restore harmony to their fractured
family. But as the Trevain family
gathers for Sir Harry's funeral,
tensions are already surfacing. Then,
at the funeral, a handsome stranger
arrives from America claiming to be
Sir Harry's grandson. The family is
outraged, but Daisy, true to her
promise to her grandfather, wel-
comes the stranger to Pencreek and
finds herself irresistibly drawn to
Ben Trevain . . .

JOYCE JOHNSON

CUCKOO IN THE NEST

Complete and Unabridged

LINFORD
Leicester

First published in Great Britain in 2008

First Linford Edition
published 2009

British Library CIP Data

Johnson, Joyce, *1931* –
    Cuckoo in the nest- -(Linford romance library)
    1. Grandfathers- -Death- -Fiction.
    2. Family- -Fiction.
    3. Love stories.
    4. Large type books.
    I. Title II. Series
    823.9′14–dc22

ISBN 978–1–84782–757–9

The End of An Era

Daisy Trevain took up her position by the restaurant's front door to see her last party booking safely off the premises. The Pencreek Ladies' Supper Club, genial and relaxed after a great meal plus a generous supply of Daisy's finest wine, were noisily collecting bags and coats, chattering and calling to each other like a flock of starlings. They lingered to confirm the date of the next meeting, to exchange last bits of village gossip they'd missed during the evening. They were in no hurry to leave the cosy warmth of the Harbourside Bistro to face the squalls outside.

'All ready?' Daisy had her hand on the heavy iron latch and flung open the door. 'Goodnight, ladies, hope to see you again soon. Take care out there — it's a horrid night.'

'See you next month, Daisy. Lovely meal.'

Daisy stood by the lighted doorway until the last of them were swallowed up in the darkness, then thankfully closed the heavy oak door, one of the inn's original 18th century fittings.

'Are you there, Rosie?' she called out. 'They've gone — at last!'

Rosie, her friend and the restaurant's manageress, came into the main dining-room. 'It's all tidy in the kitchen. They certainly all enjoyed their eating and that's really what counts.'

'They're great customers. It's locals like the Supper Club and other village groups and clubs that keep us going in the winter. You look tired, Rosie — go home now.'

'I'm fine. I'll give you a hand clearing up. The kitchen staff have gone. Martin's anxious about his wife — the baby's due any time.'

'He did a great job tonight — that chocolate pudding!'

'Yes, I had a sample. It was fab! Shall

I make us coffee?'

'No thanks, I'll finish up here first. Off you go — and take care going home. Don't go along by the harbour.'

'No fear, I'll take the back lane. Piran will be looking out for me. I'll phone him on my mobile. You've locked the front door?'

'Of course. I'll lock the back after you.'

'OK. See you tomorrow.' The two girls hugged a fond farewell.

Daisy and Rosie had been friends since babyhood and had gone to the village school together. When Daisy was sent to a private boarding school their ways had parted, but she had always spent the long summer holidays at home and kept up with her local friends. In their early twenties both had returned to roost in their beloved home nests in the Cornish fishing village of Pencreek, but jobs were few in the local area.

Rosie had left to work in the city for a while but had returned to marry her childhood sweetheart, fisherman Piran Randall. Neither she nor Piran wanted to leave the area so it had been a heaven-sent opportunity when Daisy had opened the Harbourside Bistro and had asked Rosie to be manageress. Daisy had been equally grateful to have the solid support of her friend, a hard-working gem who could turn her hand to anything.

Alone in the bistro Daisy tidied up, dimmed the lights and checked the very satisfactory takings. Next step, upstairs to her lovely cosy flat, a long luxurious soak, and finally supper leftovers and a glass of wine.

'Heaven,' she breathed, well content with life, one foot on the first step. Then she froze as a voice reached her ears.

'Daisy, Daisy, your light's on, I know you're up!' The voice was accompanied by knocks on her back door. 'Open up, Daisy. It's about tomorrow's fish orders. Let me in, it's sleeting down here.'

There was nothing else for it. She

went back through the kitchen to the back door where it was comparatively sheltered, but even there the door was almost wrenched out of her grip by the wind. She had to struggle to keep it open until her muscular visitor threw his weight against it.

'Quick — inside, Dave, it's tipping down. You're wet through.'

Dave Bunt shook his head, sending raindrops splattering on to the shining clean work surfaces.

'Here.' Daisy threw him a towel. 'I'll put the kettle on. You look frozen. You surely haven't been out at sea tonight?'

'Of course not, we Bunts don't have a death wish even though it breaks Dad's heart to miss a tide. Usually he sits in the pub all night with his half pint, chuntering on about his starving family.'

'Aw, poor Jem.'

'Poor nothing, Dad's as rich as Croesus what with his fleet of holiday boats and the fishing — though Brian and I do most of that.' He rubbed his dark head vigorously, damp curls springing around his flushed face. 'Anyhow, the harbour chains are up so it would be some fool who'd put to see on a night like this.'

'Here — ' Daisy poured a tot of whisky into his coffee mug ' — dry out a bit before you go. You're very late — you've no fish today, surely?'

'Not caught fresh, but you know we keep a good stock in the freezer. It wouldn't do to let our regulars down. And I'm late because Dad dragooned Brian and me into his net-mending in the sheds.'

'Well, good for you. We could have managed, of course, but Martin loves his fish specials. So thanks, Dave, it was very thoughtful of you.'

'It's not that late. 'Tis often two or three in the morning in the season. And besides . . . ' He floundered, stopped, then took a gulp of coffee before looking Daisy straight in the eye.

Her heart sank. She was very fond of Dave, a good friend from infant school days and a wonderful source of fresh Cornish fish for the bistro specials. They made a good business partnership, but she'd had an inkling lately that he was looking for a more meaningful relationship. But she was too busy even to contemplate anything like that, *and*, truth to tell, wary. Relationships in her own family background were not significant examples of marital bliss. For the present she was enjoying the challenge of being her own person.

Quickly she took his empty mug from the counter.

'It's pretty late, and I've been up since dawn, with an early start again tomorrow, so — I've written a provisional fish order just in case you looked in.' She handed him a list. 'Do what you can and we'll adapt our menu accordingly.'

But Dave didn't even look at it. He leaned on the counter.

'Er . . . I've been thinking, maybe you and I . . . there's a new club opened over at Newquay . . . '

'Um . . . yes. Rosie and I were talking about it earlier. Perhaps we should make up a party one week when we're both off. We could get the gang together before the season starts, maybe hire a minibus.'

'No, no.' He shook his head. 'I didn't mean a party. Just you and . . . '

The phone ringing stopped him in his tracks. He looked at his watch and frowned. 'It's late for a call, isn't it?'

'Ssh.' Daisy held up her hand to shush him as she grabbed the phone. This late, it could be only one thing.

'Yes,' she said tersely. 'Yes, it's Daisy — no, I'm still up . . . What? Granny, what is it?' As she listened her eyes closed and her hand flew to her mouth. 'Oh, Granny, no . . . Yes, I know, but . . . ' There was a sob in her voice, and her eyes widened. 'Right now, do you mean?'

Dave moved closer, questioning, but she put her finger to her lips.

'OK, Gran. I'll come right over. No, no, the wind's died a bit,' she lied.

'Don't worry, I'll be with you in less than half an hour. Is there anyone else there with you? No sign of Dad yet? OK, see you soon.'

As soon as she hung up, Dave spoke. 'What is it? Your grandfather? He's very ill, folks say. No-one's seen him for ages. Are you going up to the Hall? I'll take you. The storm's worsening, not getting better, and it's dangerous out there.'

'It's good of you to offer, but I'll be staying over . . . what's left of the night. Granny sounded terrible — usually she can cope with anything.'

'No family there?'

'My dad's in Las Vegas, probably on the lookout for a new bride — that'll be number three. The rest are out of the country or out of sight.'

'Sounds bad. Do you . . . ?'

'Don't worry, I'll be all right. You know, Dave, my gran and grandad have been in *loco parentis* . . . well, until Grandad . . . ' She shook her head. 'Come on, I'm wasting time. It's a long story. I'm sure the village gossips know it all!'

The whole village knew about Sir Harry Trevain: rags to riches, village boy made good, his heyday in the 80s and 90s amassing a massive fortune, which was now on the slide as he became more and more reclusive, leaving his warring relatives squabbling over his empire.

'Is he — is your grandad . . ?' Dave asked tentatively as Daisy scribbled notes to Rosie and Martin.

'He's very ill. Could you make sure Rosie gets this note? I'll phone in the morning.' A rattle of hail on the window punctuated her words.

'I have to go now.' She threw her car keys to Dave. 'Be an angel and get my car for me. It's in Piran's garages — number three.'

Parking was a permanent problem in the village's narrow streets and garage-less dwellings. Rosie's husband, Piran, had inherited some old fish sheds from an uncle and had turned them into money-spinning garages. Daisy was lucky to have a 'good friends discount.'

'Are you sure I can't take you? The van's outside and I could pick you up tomorrow when you're ready . . . '

'Thanks, but no. I'm better under my own steam. I'm not sure what's happening exactly. Just a tick — I must remind Rosie about tomorrow night's party . . . '

'Don't fuss, Daisy. The Harbourside Bistro's too popular to fall apart just because you're not there in the morning.'

'I know, I know, but it's my baby and a much-loved one.' She smiled and Dave's heart fluttered.

'Let me take you,' he pleaded.

'No. I have to go and see what's happening and I need to be a free agent. Things aren't right at the Hall. Grandad only wants me, not even Granny. All his meals are put outside his door. It's . . . kind of scary.' She shivered. 'I must go. Two minutes to pack a bag and I'll be ready.'

Daisy swiftly packed an overnight bag, and was at the door when Dave drew up in her car.

He got out and yelled above the shrieking wind, 'You shouldn't go alone. There are too many trees on the way to the Hall — you could find the road blocked. Let me come with you.'

'Then there would be two of us at risk. That's not very sensible. Thanks anyway, but go home now.' She slammed the door, revved the engine, switched on the lights, and waved to Dave who was still standing by his van, an exasperated expression on his face.

Mouthing 'Go home,' she depressed the accelerator.

★ ★ ★

Her 4 × 4 was heavy and powerful but even that vehicle swayed before the tempest as rain sheeted across the windscreen, blurring her vision.

On a night like this there weren't many vehicles on the road out of the

12

village. She met only one other car as she swung on to the main road leading to Trevain Hall where her grandparents lived. She drove cautiously, on the lookout for fallen trees and floodwaters, concentrating on the road, trying not to think about her gran's anxiety on the phone. Martha Trevain was not a woman to panic and would never have brought her out on such a night without a very good reason.

There was family ostensibly living in the Hall; her Uncle Christopher and Aunt Patricia lived in a flat in the east wing, but they were often away for weeks at a time. Christopher Trevain's role was to oversee some of the business his father Harry had built up over the years, though Daisy knew from her aunt that he spent more time checking out golf courses than the now ailing businesses.

Occasionally other family branches drifted in and out of the Hall, waiting for poor old Grandad to die, thought Daisy uncharitably as she drove along a stretch of woodland road. Trees creaked and groaned alarmingly, and she barely managed to skirt round a substantial branch partially blocking the road.

Once clear of the trees she was on the final short run to the Hall. The rain had eased a little but dark clouds still scudded threateningly across the night sky and she was relieved to reach the iron gates protecting Trevain Hall's sweeping parklands. The gates stood open.

Lights shone from several rooms of the stately Hall, an old Georgian manor house lovingly restored thirty years earlier when the Trevain family fortunes had been at their peak. Daisy loved the house, her home for well over twenty years, yet she couldn't help noticing its growing shabbiness, its once immaculate grounds now not quite so immaculate; even her grand-mother's beloved rose garden was neglected and unpruned.

She parked by the imposing front door, and as she ran up the steps the door swung open.

'Daisy, my dear girl, thank God you're safe. I'm so sorry . . . ' A handsome, elderly woman with thick silvery hair clasped Daisy to her. 'Come in, come in. Molly's left a fire in the library, with coffee and sandwiches, too. I'm sorry to bring you out on such a night, but . . . ' she set off at a great pace down a long corridor ' . . . your grandfather . . . '

'Slow down, Gran, I can hardly keep up with you! Is there no-one else here? I thought you'd sent for my dad?'

'I did, but apparently he's 'tied up'. His words, whatever that means. In any case, you know how Harry feels about him. He won't have anyone near him except you.' She stopped for breath as she opened the library door. 'There, Molly's lit the fire. Wasn't that kind?'

Smoke billowed back from the chimneypiece, hovered round the room and settled over a small table laid out with sandwiches and coffee. Daisy and her grandmother coughed and

15

spluttered, Martha waving her arms at the smoke.

'Shut the door, quickly! The chimney needs sweeping. Come and warm yourself, it's chilly in here.'

'But Grandad . . . ' Daisy was bewildered. 'How is he? Shouldn't I go and see . . . ?'

'Oh, he's very poorly. The doctor's been. I can't do any more.' She poked the fire, her back to Daisy, and when she turned her eyes were tear-filled. 'He barely tolerates me. He had a very bad turn earlier — he was quite raving. He was desperate to see you — kept calling your name, rambling on about America.'

'Shouldn't I go and . . . '

'Presently. The doctor gave him a sedative . . . to calm him down. He was . . . rather wild. He tried to get up, to get dressed, saying he was coming to see you, so Dr Ross gave him a knockout dose. But he may wake at any time and that's why I asked you to bring an overnight bag.' She sighed,

16

pushing her hair back from her face. 'I don't think he'll last much longer, Daisy, but I fear there's something terrible on his mind that he wants to tell us about, and I've no idea what it is.'

* * *

Howling winds buffeted the thick stone walls of Trevain Hall but deep inside the building the library was deathly quiet. Martha Trevain stared intently at the leaping flames as though to find the answers to the questions of her troubled mind.

'Granny — ' Daisy touched Martha's arm ' — perhaps we should try again to contact my dad, Uncle Peter . . . '

'No, no, not yet. They know the score but . . . ' she swallowed ' . . . your grandfather doesn't want them, only you. I've tried to find out why he won't see his sons . . . but I can't help him, not since he shut himself in that apartment, as far away from the main

17

house as possible.'

'But . . .'

'No, it's no good, Daisy, I've tried everything.'

'You should have called me earlier.'

'No.' A wry smile touched Martha's lips. 'Even though he's so sick he was smart enough to insist that you didn't leave your bistro until closing time. I'm sorry, you must be worn out.'

'I'm fine. Shouldn't we . . . I'll go and see him now, shall I?'

'In a while. The sedative Dr Ross gave him should last a little longer.' Martha busied herself pouring coffee. 'I'm afraid Dr Ross said he could go at any time.'

'So we should get the rest of the family?'

'Definitely not. He won't see them. He goes into a rage if I mention them.' Martha bit her lip, struggling to overcome the emotion. 'I hate to say it, Daisy, but our boys have been a dreadful disappointment to him.'

'That's terrible. His own sons. But

they're not so bad, surely? I know Dad went off the rails when Mum died — he's hardly been a role model for me, but I've always had you and Grandad. I've been so lucky.'

'Bless you.' Martha hugged her. 'And you've given us nothing but pleasure. You were always the apple of your grandad's eye.' She put a guard round the fire before turning to face the girl. 'Do you remember much about Harriet, your mother?'

'Not a lot.' Memory flashed. 'A snatch of lullaby, a sort of fragrance — her perfume, I suppose — a soft voice, but no, not much at all . . . and after she died Dad was hardly ever here.'

'Ah well,' Martha said briskly, 'that's the past. Maybe we should confront the present right now.' She checked the guard again. 'Let's go and see your grandfather.'

Martha led her back to the hall, then down a long winding corridor to the other side of the house, a darker, gloomier side, originally the servants' quarters in the Trevains' grander days. Now only faithful Molly from the village came on a daily basis and Sam, her husband, coped as best he could with the ever-encroaching garden. They stopped before the heavy oak door which led to Harry Trevain's own apartment, an apartment he had never left for well over a year, shunning his family and the outside world. Molly and Daisy were his only visitors; Martha he tolerated for short intervals. He gave no reasons.

At first there had been some concern, but gradually the family had shrugged their collective shoulders and got on with their own lives. In his sons' young days Harry, pursuing global business interests, had been very much an absent father. Now he refused point-blank to see any of his family except Daisy and, occasionally, one of her younger cousins, Guy Trevain.

Outside his rooms, Martha hesitated. 'Maybe we should wait until morning?'

'No,' Daisy insisted. 'And he should have someone with him surely? Nursing care? He's a long way from the main house.'

'It's his choice. I offered, but he refused. He has an alarm and panic buttons, and a mobile phone.' Martha opened the door. 'He can contact Dr Ross any time.'

The room was dark, and quite cold; a single shaded lamp on a bedside table gave a dim light. Bottles and pill boxes cluttered the table top.

Daisy shivered and looked around for some heating.

Martha pre-empted Daisy's question. 'He won't have a fire — says it's too hot.' She moved to the bedside. 'Harry, it's Daisy to see you. She came through the storm.'

An eyelid flickered and there was a small hand movement towards Daisy. Daisy took his hand. 'I'm here, Grandad.'

'Daisy!' There was a faint but firmer grasp, then his eyes opened and he

21

struggled to sit upright.

'Don't move.' She sat on the bed but he continued to struggle, peering round the dimly-lit room.

'Who's there?' he asked sharply. 'Behind you, there!'

'It's Granny — she's worried . . . '

He waved an arm. 'Go away! Just Daisy. No-one else. Go, Martha.' His face contorted and his breathing shortened.

'All right, Harry, I'm going. I just wanted to know how you were feeling,' Martha said soothingly.

All she got for her sympathy were an exasperated sigh and a dismissive gesture as to a child nuisance.

'OK,' Martha whispered to Daisy, 'I'll come back later.'

'You should go to bed,' Daisy advised. 'Don't worry, I'll stay with Grandad.'

'There's a blanket on the chair. I hope he sleeps. Call me if . . . '

'I will. Go now.' Daisy hugged her grandmother. 'I'll be fine.'

Martha nodded and like a shadow left the room.

Daisy arranged herself more comfortably in a bedside chair and took her grandfather's hand.

'Now, tell me, what is it, Grandad?'

'Bistro?' His voice was a little stronger as he asked what was always his first question. 'How's business.'

'Fine. Great tonight, actually, in spite of the awful weather.'

He gave a pleased sigh, and a hint of a smile, but Daisy's heart contracted. He looked so ill, so haggard, his papery skin blotched with brown age spots, his breath a mere rasp. Yet she saw beyond the sad trappings of his age. She saw a younger, tall, strong man who carried her on his back, or swung her up into his arms, playing children's games, then later teaching her tennis, swimming, sailing, financing her business venture, encouraging, beaming approval, always ready with sound advice. Tears welled as she leaned over to kiss him.

'You've always been there for me,

such a support. Thank you.'

He touched her hair. 'I've been thinking — the bistro — you could expand to a chain of Harbourside Bistros, a countrywide franchise . . . ' His voice faded and he sank back, eyes closed.

Daisy pulled the rug more closely round her shoulders. Typical Grandad, she thought lovingly — national Harbourside Bistros indeed! He was missing the point. The whole essence of the bistro was its sense of locality. Her bistro was unique.

And yet, he was usually right where business was concerned. She would think about it. It was quite tempting . . . a challenge!

She snuggled into her blanket, her drifting thoughts turning to a dream: each bistro with its own unique local flavour, regional menus . . . Her head nodded and sleep reached for her.

★ ★ ★

It could only have been a few moments'
light doze before she woke to a cry.
Harry was shaking violently, struggling
to speak, to breathe, his eyes wide open.
She took a glass of water from the table
and tried to offer it to him, but he
pushed it away, shaking his head.

'No! No . . . Martha . . . ?'

'I'll get her.' Daisy made for the door.

'No. No . . . you, Daisy . . . must see
to it . . . him, too . . . be hard . . . you
must help him . . . the others . . . ' He
had to fight for every breath, yet he
clutched her arm so tightly that she
knew she would carry the bruise for
days. Then he shook her arm so
violently that she cried out. At that he
released her and took her hand more
gently.

'Sorry. Daisy, I did it all wrong. You
set it right. Promise . . . harmony . . . '

Harry was fighting for breath with
shuddering gasps and now Daisy was
really frightened. She tried to pull him
upright and he clutched at her, his eyes
now unclouded.

'See, Daisy, it'll be all right now. Promise me, promise, Daisy — peace and harmony — a family team.'

'Yes, yes, Grandad, I promise. I swear.'

'Thank you, Daisy, dear, dear girl. Put it right . . . tell Martha . . . tell Martha . . . ' His eyes closed and Daisy felt his grip releasing her arm . . .

Some instinct had brought Martha running upstairs, and she came into the room just as Daisy was closing her mobile phone.

'Oh, Gran, I'm so sorry . . . I've called Dr Ross.' Daisy stood helplessly by as Martha went to her husband's side.

Martha nodded, holding Harry's hand. 'He will come but there's no need. Whatever was troubling my dear Harry is of no account now. He's at peace now. He's suffered so these last years.'

Daisy said nothing. Her grandfather's last moment had been anything but peaceful but it would be cruel to share that knowledge with Martha.

'Go to bed, Granny,' she said gently. 'I'll stay until Dr Ross comes.'

'No, you must be worn out. It'll be dawn soon. Get some sleep and let me be alone with your grandfather for a while.' Martha smiled at her through tear-filled eyes. 'I've so much to be grateful for, so leave me to remember our happier times together. I'll be fine now. Really.'

Daisy kissed her, then, after a last look at her grandfather and a final kiss on his forehead, she slipped out of the room.

Dr Ross came and went. Martha refused a sedative, preferring to keep vigil by her husband's side until clear light of day.

Daisy slept heavily until Molly came into her room to pull back the curtains with a rattle.

'Sorry, my dear, but 'tis near noon. I've brought you tea. Lady Trevain's up — never slept at all, I'd guess, poor soul. I'm so sorry about Sir Harry,

27

though 'tis truly a blessing. It's broke my heart lately seeing such a change in a man. Lovely he was in the old days — always a word for us and sweets for the children, too. He'll be missed hereabouts.'

Daisy sipped her tea. 'Thanks, Molly, that's just what I needed. How's Gran?'

'Sort of resigned. She's been on the phone to your dad and your Uncle Peter. Your dad's in Las Vegas, your Uncle Peter's on the Riviera, and your Aunt Patricia and Uncle Christopher are in the Caribbean — for the golf, I imagine. Oh, and Rosie phoned — you're not to worry, they're managing fine at the bistro without you.'

'That's good. Oh, Molly, that sun!' She got out of bed and went to the window. Golden sun, dazzling vanquisher of the storms; clear, deep blue sky; and away on the horizon the sharp grey line of the channel. It was such a contrast to yesterday — and then, suddenly, the tears flowed. She sat on her bed and sobbed out her sorrow.

'There, me dear,' Molly patted her shoulder, 'you cry all you want. 'Tis a hard loss but you've been a wonderful maid to your grandfather. He was so proud of you. 'Molly,' he'd say, 'that young Daisy has more sense in her little finger than all my blasted boys put together.' '

'Oh, don't, Molly. He's been wonderful to me . . . setting me up in the bistro . . . ' She wiped her eyes, blew her nose.

'It's time to repay, then.' Molly folded towels, threw back the bed covers. 'Lady Trevain's going to need you. You'll have to be strong.'

'I know, and I will be, but right now I feel so alone. I can't believe Grandad's gone'

'Well, dear girl, that's life — it's all part of the pattern, so maybe it's up to you to straighten out the pattern.'

'What do you mean? What pattern?'

Molly shrugged and gave the duvet a vigorous shake. 'It's not my place to say, but you Trevains, barring yourself, her ladyship and maybe young Guy, you're not exactly . . . well, what I'd call harmonious. Not like some families,' she finished hastily.

'Huh.' Daisy looked curiously at Molly. 'How do you mean? You think we're what they call dysfunctional?'

'I wouldn't know about that. Maybe I shouldn't have spoken out but I've known you all for such a long time. I remember you and your dad coming here after your poor mam died — tragic that was. Since then things haven't . . . ' Confused, she stopped and looked anxiously at Daisy. 'Sorry.'

'No, no, you shouldn't be.' Daisy flung her arms around Molly. 'No, you're the gem in the basket. We're *not* a proper family, we're always squabbling over something. Our roots are here in the village but we've mostly fled to other parts of the world. Maybe that's what Grandad meant by harmony — Trevain harmony. He wants me to pull the family back together, bring them home, back to their roots.'

Molly looked a little bewildered. 'I'm not so sure what you mean.'

'Never mind, it's just a thought. Give me ten minutes in the shower and I'll be ready for action, to set the ball rolling and gather up the Trevain clan. Thank you. Thank you, Molly!'

As Daisy turned the shower on, Molly smoothed out the bed covers and gave the pillows a shake before placing them carefully at precise angles above the duvet. A worried frown creased her face and superstitiously she raised her eyes heavenwards.

'Oh, goodness, Sir Harry, I don't quite understand but I'm sure you didn't mean for that poor maid to start on that Herculean task all by herself. Poor Miss Daisy. Why can't I keep my big mouth shut?'

The Family Gathers

News of Sir Harry Trevain's death spread rapidly through the small fishing village of his birthplace before it spread tentacles through, first, the county, then nationwide, meriting a brief biographical slot on the local TV news. A full obituary in the national Press would cover Sir Harry's life from its humble beginnings in the West Country to his global achievements.

By evening there were scores of floral tributes left at the Hall gates and many messages of sympathy for the family. Flags flew at half-mast, while one or two local businesses who owed their own modest successes to Sir Harry closed for half a day. Daisy considered closing the bistro, but she knew her business-minded grandad would have scoffed at the notion of losing business. Indeed, drinks on the house to salute his passing would possibly have been a more appropriate measure in his eyes.

Martha and Daisy were almost too busy to grieve in the immediate aftermath of the death: letters, phone calls and funeral arrangements kept them fully occupied. Daisy was amazed at the sheer volume of messages and commentary. Sir Harry's personal and business dealings were spread widely across the globe, from selling fish on Pencreek's harbour quay to being in control of a large financial empire.

As the funeral date was fixed the Trevain family members began to make their way to Trevain Hall; sons, grandsons, distant cousins, and great grandsons, great nephews and nieces, and distant relatives Daisy had hardly heard of. Solicitors from a well-known London firm and Sir Harry's old friend and local lawyer Charlie Liddicoat were closeted with Martha for a morning, and there was much speculation about the contents of Sir Harry's will.

In life he had helped many of his

relatives, both close and distant, as well as friends. His fortune was known to be vast in spite of the eccentricity of his final years, and there was the question of whether his latest will was a product of those late years, when his mental capacity had been suspect, or of his benign philanthropic years.

Daisy's father, Jack Trevain, was one of the last to arrive. Daisy picked him up at the station, but for a moment she didn't recognise him. It was well over a year since she'd seen him briefly in London but he now looked at least ten years older.

'Daisy dear.' He embraced her warmly. 'I'm glad to see you.'

She noticed he was thinner, greyer, almost ill looking. 'Are you all right, Dad? Why didn't you come home sooner?'

He shrugged. 'I came the long way round. I couldn't afford direct flights.'

'And where's . . . er . . . Jude?'

'I left her in London. Family things are hardly her scene. Anyway, I wanted to see you, and Mum, of course. How is she? And Peter? Is my brother still looking for his rich heiress?'

'Probably. We don't see him much, but they're all assembled for the funeral. My car's parked over there. Where's your luggage?'

'Here.' He swung a holdall towards her.

'Is that all? Aren't you staying?'

'That depends. Quite frankly, Daisy, it all depends on how the old man's . . . um, divided up the assets.'

'Dad!' Daisy was shocked.

'There's no need to be like that. We all know you were the apple of his eye, but surely he won't have cut his own sons out of his will. Or has he?'

'I honestly haven't thought about it, we've been so busy, Gran and I.'

'Well, he's set you up all right. The Harbourside Bistro, is it? It must be a gold mine in this part of tourist England.'

'It's hard work, and I pay Grandad rent. I'm paying off the loan.'

'But he'll have left you a packet?'

'I don't know and I don't much care. Please, Dad, don't talk about it. He wasn't happy in his last years, and you never came home to see him. It was horrid.' Tears began to blind her. After all the grief and tensions of the last days, all her father could talk about was the will and money!

'Daisy, I'm sorry. I didn't mean all that. Life hasn't been rosy for me lately, but I'd no right to . . . Come on, let me drive. I reckon I still know the way back to the family mansion, just about. Cheer up, love. I'll stay home for a while this time.' He put his arms around her and she was momentarily comforted, although she couldn't help a frisson of unease about the impending funeral and the days and weeks thereafter.

★ ★ ★

In the days following Sir Harry Trevain's death family members from all parts had begun to assemble for the funeral. As with many large families there had been rivalries, quarrels and disagreements, the main causes long forgotten, but hurt feelings remaining through pride or sheer stubbornness.

Aware of possible tension in the charged atmosphere of an important funeral such as Sir Harry's where a large inheritance was at stake, Martha and Daisy planned a formal dinner in the evening before the funeral for as many Trevains as wished to attend. Daisy had commissioned the Harbourside Bistro chef, Martin, and his staff to put on the meal, hoping it would be a talking point and a diversion from potential arguments. The big dining-room, capable of holding some forty guests, had been dusted down and polished for the event.

Half an hour before the dinner Daisy and Martha met to check the long table now set with the best Trevain silver and crystal.

'Harry would have approved,' Martha

said sadly as she aligned cutlery to a perfect symmetry. 'He used to love the formal dinners we gave — summer balls, garden parties, Hunt dinners, even concerts when he was going through his musical evenings phase.'

Daisy put her arm round her granny's shoulders. 'I'm sorry, was this a mistake? Too sad, maybe, too many memories . . . '

'No, of course not, those are happy memories, and this preparation takes my mind off the future, a future I dread without Harry, even though the last years . . . ' She stopped, compressed her lips.

'What?' said Daisy as Martha's eyes clouded.

'Nothing. I've had a good life with Harry. I've never wanted for a thing and I'm grateful for that.' She touched a couple of floral centrepieces, straightened a napkin, counted chairs. 'Gracious, thirty one! I hope we've catered for that number.'

'Of course, it's my job, remember?

Martin's in his element and so are Rosie and her staff. They're loving the chance for a peep inside the Hall! It'll be fine.'

Martha still looked worried. 'Maybe we should have had the dinner *after* the funeral.'

'I'm sure we shouldn't.' Daisy was decisive; she saw possible problems after the funeral and the formal reading of the will, which her grandfather had apparently requested. She had no idea what it contained, but her father's bitter outburst had unsettled her. How many others were expecting Sir Harry to have remembered them? He'd shown little interest in any of his relatives in the last few years.

'This is best,' she reaffirmed. 'Then just afternoon tea after the funeral.'

Martha gave an inelegant snort. 'Huh! I can't see the Trevain men sticking to tea. Peter and your father are already making inroads into their father's best malt. I saw them in the library — they looked like they were having an argument. Your father doesn't look too well. Has he spoken to you, Daisy?'

'Er . . . he just said that things haven't been going too well lately.'

'Oh, dear. Has he brought what's-her-name . . . Samantha . . . with him? I haven't seen her around.'

'No, Sam was his last wife — she divorced him four years ago.'

'Oh, that's a shame, I quite liked her. Who's the latest?'

'Jude, apparently, but she's not here — she doesn't 'do' funerals.'

Martha raised her eyebrows heavenwards. 'Oh, Lord, where did we go so wrong with our boys?'

'You didn't. Dad's OK really,' Daisy said loyally. 'He was knocked off course by Mum's death when they'd only been married for three years. Uncle Peter — well, he's just been a merry widower for years, and he's still looking for a rich heiress.'

'All boys,' Martha mused. 'Not a Trevain girl for generations, except you,

Daisy. Harry worshipped you. He believed the male Trevains were cursed — bad blood, punishment for past sins.'

'That's rubbish. You've lived in this big, dark old house for too long. In fact, at the end of the season I'm going to take you away. Sunshine, blue skies — that's what you need. We'll do the sights, the grand tour. You've hardly left Cornwall for years.'

'I know. That would be wonderful. Harry was always too busy to take me on his trips — said I'd be bored in any case. He had so many business meeting. But *your* business, Daisy, the bistro, you couldn't leave it.'

'I'll worry about that when the time comes. That's one valuable lesson among many I learned from Grandad: if you set up a business on the right lines from the start, it'll stand on its own when necessary, and I've a great staff. So, it's a date, September or October, the Grand Tour — Australia, Canada, California . . . '

'Whoa, one thing at a time.' Martha

glanced at her watch. 'Let's get this over with before we make any plans. I'm sure Rosie will be sounding the pre-dinner gong soon. We'd best join the others.'

Only afterwards did it occur to Daisy to wonder why Harry had never taken Martha with him on his frequent business trips, especially to the States, which she had always wanted to visit.

As the pre-dinner gong sounded, Martha put her hand to her mouth. 'Can I do this, Daisy? Harry . . . '

'You can, and Grandad would have been proud of you. Apart from your sad eyes you look lovely.'

'This was Harry's favourite dress. I'm too old for it really, and midnight blue chiffon is a bit passé . . . '

'Not a bit of it, and with your lovely white hair . . . Come on, let's face the music and round up the Trevain clan. I think most of them are in the sitting-room, but we'll check the library on the way.' She linked arms as they moved out of the dining-room towards the assembly of Trevains.

★ ★ ★

There was no one in the library and a reassuringly civilized buzz from the spacious sitting-room. Arthur, loaned from the bistro staff, was doing a brisk pre-dinner drinks service.

There was a respectful hush as Martha came into the room, as though everyone felt guilty to be enjoying a pre-funeral event, but as she smiled at them encouragingly, conversation was resumed.

'That gong was a ten-minute warning.' She spoke clearly, well in control. 'We must move into the dining-room promptly on the next one.'

'That's pretty feudal stuff,' a disgruntled voice said from the back. It was George Trevain, one of Harry's grandsons.

'Not really,' Martha said sweetly. 'Your grandad would have appreciated it. There's no harm in a little tradition.'

43

'Quite right, so shut up for once, George.' A tall, dark-haired young man came to kiss Martha and Daisy. 'Hi, Gran, I think this evening's a brilliant idea. Can I get you a drink?'

'A small one, dear. Thank you.'

'For you, Daisy?' Guy Trevain, George's brother, was a business student, best and brightest of the current Trevain young men. He made no secret of his admiration for Daisy, and she remained his mentor, confidante, best friend and very favourite relative.

'Not just now thanks, Guy — later, perhaps, when dinner's under way.' She touched his shoulder affectionately. 'I'm dreading this,' she murmured.

'Don't worry, it'll go great. I've been circulating,' he confided. 'They aren't so bad, though some I've never met . . . '

'I know. Grandad had a lot of siblings, scattered through England and beyond. I often wonder . . . ' But the gong banged again, this time with a sense of urgency.

'Right,' Martha beckoned, 'dining-room please, everyone.'

She ushered her guests across the great hall and into the large panelled dining-room. There were gasps of admiration at the sight of the gleaming silver, immaculate porcelain, and dazzling damask.

'Wow!' Guy said to Daisy. 'Impressive! I've never seen it like this.'

'I have vague memories of peeping through the banisters when I was a tiny girl, creeping to the door, and being carried back to bed . . . This is a special effort for Sir Harry. He loved it like this in the old days. Please, everyone,' she raised her voice and clapped her hands, 'sit where you want — we thought it best to be as informal as possible.'

She lowered her voice. 'Oh-oh, Guy, we've got a problem already, Uncle Peter and my dad on either side of Granny — glaring across like turkey cocks.'

'Your gran'll control them, but I'll

45

nip in and get a seat nearby. See you later.'

On the whole the informal approach seemed to be working. There was a friendly buzz as people found seats, unfolded napkins with hungry anticipation, and explained their Trevain connections to their fellow diners, and Daisy began to breathe more easily as the meal proceeded. Chef Martin's crab soup was a satisfying starter and the guests began to relax, but as more wine went round Daisy knew her relief would be short-lived. Her Uncle Peter, in his mid-sixties, was some twenty years senior to his brother, Jack, who had been a late surprise baby to Martha and Harry. They had never got on.

Peter was glaring at his younger brother. 'You took your time getting here. You arrived when everything was done.'

'Done? You should talk! You were in Portugal swanning round the golf courses until a day or so ago. My Daisy and Mother had to do everything. And you should never have gone away anyway, with Dad so poorly and . . . '

'Huh, and where were you? You've never been near since . . . '

'Boys!' Martha snapped. 'For goodness' sake, think why you're here.'

'I know why Peter is here,' Jack returned quickly. 'He's out for . . . '

Guy quickly leaned across his neighbour. 'Uncle Jack, your favourite course is coming up next — a batch of John Dory fish from the family market. Hey, Dad?' He appealed to his father, Christopher Trevain, one of the few working Trevain men. Harry Trevain had put his son Christopher in charge of the once lucrative fish business, a spin-off from Harry's own beginnings selling fish to locals on Pencreek's quay. Now the business served the South West and beyond for both small exclusive retail outlets and the large wholesale and restaurant trade.

Christopher was an amiable, intelligent, but lazy, man, content to let the business tick over for a small profit, though lately it had appeared to pick up, much to the relief of his wife, Patricia, a shrewd, handsome woman and a social climber. Now, eyes glinting, she took in every detail of the scene in the dining hall, mentally pricing the family silver.

She was desperate to know the content of Sir Harry's will, as both she and Christopher were big spenders living way beyond their means. Debts were piling up. Her son, George, was a jobless liability, while Guy was at university completing his Masters degree in Business Studies with another costly twelve months' study in America on the horizon. She knew Sir Harry had little time for his sons but surely he would provide for his grandchildren? Patricia Trevain, whatever her faults, was a good mother who loved her boys, and she wanted only the best for them.

Secretly she admired Daisy, though she considered the bistro limited and parochial. But Sir Harry had idolised his granddaughter and she would almost certainly get a sizeable chunk of his fortune. Patricia had no time for any other Trevains; she just longed for this silly evening to be over, the funeral done with and for the lawyers to reveal the share-out of the Trevain fortune.

Patricia Trevain had one wish granted. The dinner went reasonably well, with no further family outbursts, but after coffee and liqueurs in the drawing-room most guests pleaded fatigue. An early night seemed a popular option, and back in her own flat in the Hall Patricia was one step nearer to the will reading.

Daisy, Guy and George helped load the bistro equipment into the van.

'Thank you, all,' Daisy said to the bistro team. 'A success, I'd say.'

'It's surprising what a placation good food can be,' Guy observed.

'I hope tomorrow goes as well,' Daisy said. 'I don't want any upsets spoiling the day, for Grandma's sake.'

'It'll be OK, I'm sure,' said Guy. 'The Trevains may be an awkward lot at times but there's too much respect for Grandad for them to fall out at his funeral.'

'I hope you're right.'

Guy patted her shoulder. 'Come on, Daisy, it's not like you to worry. Nothing can go wrong; you've seen to every detail.'

'The practical parts, yes. That's the easy bit. It's the people that worry me. The Trevains are volatile.'

'You're a Trevain and the most level-headed person I know, so stop worrying. It's a lovely night — let's take a calming stroll around the grounds, or we could drive to the village and call in at your bistro.'

'No, the grounds will be good. I'll just check on Granny. She's gone to bed, she was tired out. I'll join you in a tick. Sorry for fussing.' Yet she couldn't get rid of a premonition that something was going to go wrong tomorrow. She could have no possible inkling of the bombshell that was about to shake up all their lives after Harry Trevain's funeral.

★   ★   ★

Thousands of miles across the Atlantic in a small coastal town in California, Helen Thompson banged down the phone with an exasperated sigh.

'No good?' Her husband, Barrie, looked up from his newspaper. 'He did say it would be practically impossible to contact him.'

'Yes, but he finished filming a couple of days ago, he should be back in civilisation by now.'

'You know Ben, dear — some cause will have caught his imagination, perhaps some jungle tribe . . . '

'He's not in the jungle, he's in Peru, and he promised to . . . '

'Well, it can't be helped. He'll get in touch eventually.'

'I've left messages all over the place but if he doesn't contact me by tomorrow there's no help for it — I shall have to go on my own.'

Barrie Thompson put down his paper. 'Why?'

'Because it's important and because . . .' she hesitated ' . . . Ava would have wanted me to.'

'Ava's been dead for over fifteen years. What possible difference could it make now?'

'You never did understand about Ava, did you?'

'I tried.' Barrie sighed.

'I know.' Helen went to kiss her long-suffering husband. 'And you've been wonderful, but this is the end of the road, Barrie. And I have to be there. Ben should be, too, but he can follow me. I'm going to book a flight to London right now.'

'When do you propose going?'

'Tomorrow, of course.'

'So soon? And Ben?'

'The minute he contacts home, tell him to get over to Cornwall right away. I only hope he makes it in time.'

'You're going to tell him the truth at last?'

Helen gave a long sigh. 'I'm not sure. I'm just going to have to play it by ear.'

'Rather you than me, but I'm sure you'll do the right thing at the right time.'

'I hope so. But you, know, I think I'm getting a bit too old for all this. Maybe it's time to come clean at last.'

'I always said we should . . . '

Helen forestalled her husband with a kiss.

'Yes, I know, dear, and you're probably right, but we're just going to have to deal with the situation as it is right now.' She frowned. 'The thing is, I just don't want our boy to be hurt.'

'I shouldn't worry too much about that. He's not a boy now, he's a grown man, and quite capable of looking out for himself.' He paused, folded up his newspaper and looked at his wife. 'You know, we've been pretty lucky really. We've had a good life and the boy's been a great part of it. Shall I come with you? I ought to . . . '

'No. No, dear, thanks all the same. It's sweet of you but I'll be OK. Best on my own, though I do hope to goodness Ben gets there in time.'

'In time for what?'

'I don't know.' She spread her hands. 'The whole shooting match. Whatever. I'll go and get on the case right away.'

'You know best. I shall miss you, of course, but it can't be helped, it had to come sometime.'

'I know,' Helen said grimly, 'and I've been dreading this very day for years.'

The Reading of the Will

The day of Sir Harry's funeral a sea fret drifted in from the coast to make it a sad, damp day which reflected the mourners' moods as they gathered to pay their last respects.

The church was packed to capacity and a large screen and speakers relayed the service outside. The Pencreek male voice choir, founded and sponsored by Harry, sang his favourite hymns, and after the service lined the path from churchyard to graveyard.

The burial plot which Harry had bought for his parents was set apart and faced out to sea so that all the Trevain family bones could be laid to rest facing the ocean that had yielded so much to make their fortune.

After the service Martha and her sons greeted people as they came out of the church. The line was long and it was some time before the family mourners were free to follow the coffin to the burial plot. Daisy lingered behind to brief Patricia Trevain, who had volunteered for the task of shepherding the main guests back to Trevain Hall for the funeral tea.

'We shan't be long, Aunt Pat, Granny's done in. We'll join you very soon.'

'It's all under control, no need for you to worry. The last car's pulling away and I assume the bistro team are all in place, though I don't . . . ' Pat broke off. 'Who's that? That woman following the family to the grave? I thought only family were to go to the graveside.'

'That's the arrangement. Where? Oh, I see, tall woman, black trouser suit . . . '

'That's the one. Do you know her?'

'I don't think so. Pretty stylish, isn't she?'

'She's certainly not family. Try to talk to her, find out who she is.'

'OK. I'll catch you back at the Hall. The car's waiting for you, so go.'

Patricia was reluctant to leave. 'She's no-one I've seen before.'

'Auntie Pat, there are loads of people here who I've never seen before, lots of Grandad's business friends. I daresay she's wandered over here by mistake, but we'll go through the list later if it worries you, though I can't see why.'

'No, you probably can't. Just go and catch up with her, please. I can't think what she's doing here.'

Daisy quickened her step. The family was already round the open grave, the vicar commending Harry's body to the earth. She paused, her throat constricting . . .

The mysterious woman in black wiped her eyes with a large lace handkerchief and bowed her head.

Then it was all over and the Trevain family turned away to face a future without the leader of the clan.

The stranger took a final look at the grave, crumpled her handkerchief in her hand and turned away.

Daisy went to greet her. 'Hello, I'm Daisy Trevain, Sir Harry's granddaughter.'

'Yes, yes, I can see . . . '

'You can see? Have we met?'

'No. I'm sorry, I didn't mean . . . didn't mean to intrude. I must go.'

'No, please. You're American, aren't you? Did you know my grandfather?'

'Yes . . . er, I guess.' She took Daisy's hand. 'I'm sorry for your loss. Sir Harry was a fine man. You're fortunate to have had such a grandfather.' Her voice shook. Briefly she pressed Daisy's hand, then turned and almost ran up the path towards the church.

'Wait. Please come back to the house . . . ' Daisy called after her, but the woman had moved swiftly out of sight.

'Who was that?' Guy and his brother George joined her. Guy took her arm as they walked back to the church.

'I've no idea. An American. There were lots of people from the States on the guest list, mainly Grandad's business associates. Some will be up at the Hall.'

'I've seen her before,' Guy said, 'in the Dragon Hotel in town. I remember she was trying to make a call on her mobile, to America, I think, but there was some problem so the hotel put through the call for her in the end. A very elegant dark horse, eh?'

At the Hall, Patricia had done a wonderful job of receiving the guests. When Daisy and her cousins arrived, the atmosphere was relaxed, almost cheerful. The funeral had gone well, a very appropriate farewell to Sir Harry.

The bistro staff served Harry's favourite food: mini pasties, saffron cake, scones and clotted cream. There were reminiscences from home and abroad, tributes to a good citizen and local philanthropist. Wine was served but Daisy noticed that both her father and Peter were into the malt whisky again. She looked at her watch: two hours since the burial; people were beginning to make their farewells.

'Soon be over,' she whispered to her Aunt Patricia. 'Well done.'

'Now we can get down to the real business.'

'What do you mean?' Daisy frowned.

'The will, of course. I expect you're just as keen as the rest of us to learn how Harry's estate's being divided up.'

'I am not! I think it's awful! Dad's as bad. Poor Grandad's only just buried.'

'Well, you can afford to take that line, can't you? We know you're the favourite. He invested heavily in your bistro . . . '

'A loan! I'm paying back every penny.'

'That's as may be, but I'm sure Harry will have provided for us, too. Well, Christopher and the boys, of course.'

'Heavens, Pat, let's at least wait until the guests have gone before we pick over the bones. It's gruesome. And surely you won't know today anyway.

I'm not even sure who's handling the estate.'

'Don't be naïve, Daisy. Harry's solicitors are Charlie Liddicoat's firm. Charlie's dad and Harry were friends for years and I know they're here today.'

'I didn't see either Mr Charles or his brother Vincent at the funeral. Look, Aunt Patricia, a lot of people are leaving — shouldn't we . . . ?'

'See them off the premises? Of course . . . Look!' She suddenly grabbed Daisy's arm. 'It's that woman again — the woman who was at the graveside.' She stopped her husband who was passing with a drink in his hand. 'Christopher, that woman over there — who . . . ?'

'No idea, my love. I saw her in church though, at the back.'

'And at the graveside . . . and isn't that Charlie Liddicoat with her? What *is* going on? Where's Martha? Daisy, where . . . ?'

'At the front door, saying goodbye to people. I'll go and help her.'

Daisy made her escape quickly, and by the time she and Martha returned to the drawing-room only the immediate family remained. Jack and Peter were both clutching whisky glasses, Guy was reading, George was pacing restlessly.

'It's time I went, Ma,' he said with relief to Patricia when Martha and Daisy returned. 'I just waited to say goodbye to Gran.'

'You can't go, don't be stupid! The will!' his mother hissed.

'What? Now? Surely not. That's for the lawyer guys later, isn't it?'

Daisy was glad to see at least one member of the family hadn't been thinking solely of a possible inheritance during the funeral.

Martha sat down wearily. 'I think what I'd like is a nice cup of tea.'

'I'll get it,' Daisy offered at once. 'You look tired. You've done really well, though, and it went beautifully. Grandad would have been pleased.'

'Yes, I think he would, but — ' a faint smile played round her lips. ' — I've a feeling he hasn't quite finished with us yet. Charlie Liddicoat's just told me that Harry wished us all to hear the will straight after the funeral.'

Patricia nudged Daisy. 'Told you.'

'What? Now?' Peter and Jack looked up.

'I believe so. Mr Liddicoat will be here in a moment, he's just talking to — er — one of the guests. Well, now we're all here, I suggest the library as an appropriate room to hear Harry's wishes.' She turned to Daisy and whispered, 'Harry always did enjoy a good melodrama.'

'Did . . . do you know anything about the will?'

'Only that Harry will have taken care of me. As for his fortune, I don't care if he's left it to the Lifeboats or medical research. I loved him and I've always been proud to be his wife. That's enough for me.'

'Oh, Gran . . . ' Daisy's eyes filled with tears as she followed the family into the library where Molly and her husband, Sam, were waiting to help serve yet more food and tend the log fire.

'Heavens, what's she doing here?' Patricia Trevain glared at the elegant woman in black now standing by Charlie Liddicoat, the benign-looking silver-haired lawyer, as he spoke to them.

'Please be seated. I'm glad to see you all, although the occasion is a very sad one. Martha, would you come next to me, please?'

'Who . . . ?' She inclined her head towards the stranger who gave her a tentative smile.

Mr Liddicoat patted Martha's hand. 'Don't worry, I'll explain later. It'll soon be over.'

Patricia, about to protest at the presence of the non-family member, was quelled by a stern look from the lawyer. He knew exactly what she wanted to say and was not going to waste time by allowing her to do so.

So, all the Trevains fell silent as he

cleared his throat, took a sip of water, and opened the folder on the table.

'Again, many thanks for coming here today to honour our dear friend, Sir Harry Trevain. You may think this reading of his last will and testament on the actual day of the funeral somewhat . . . unusual, but then, Sir Harry was an unusual man. This . . . er, gathering was his wish and as you probably guess, all of you benefit from the will.'

Patricia Trevain frowned. There were too many people in the room for her liking.

'So.' Charlie Liddicoat coughed. 'I'll begin. Molly, Sam, I include you here — please be seated with the rest.'

'That's only right and proper,' Patricia whispered to her husband. 'They've looked after Harry and Martha very well. A small legacy is their due.'

Daisy noted it was six o'clock when the lawyer started to speak, and the first bequest was for Martha Trevain to be well provided for, with outright possession of Trevain Hall and a substantial annuity. Molly and Sam were similarly generously pensioned off.

The relatives looked expectant, but the lawyer then dealt with a long list of charitable gifts and bequests. By six-thirty people were beginning to fidget and look at their watches. George was almost nodding off when suddenly Mr Liddicoat caught their attention.

' 'The remaining Trevains',' he read, and there followed a list of names. ' 'To each of the aforementioned, the sum of five thousand pounds, plus, to Guy Trevain, sufficient funds to complete his education, and a sum set aside for any future business venture, to be monitored by accountants Margretts and Margretts.' '

' 'My beloved granddaughter, Daisy Trevain, I release from all debts outstanding on the property The Harbourside Bistro and a sum has been set aside for any future business expansion. Daisy has my love for the

66

bright future she deserves. She has brought nothing but happiness to my dear wife Martha and myself'.'

Charlie Liddicoat paused, took off his glasses and took a long drink of water. There was stunned silence for two minutes as the Trevains digested the facts.

'And . . . ?' Peter pressed. 'Is that all? Those bequests have only nibbled around the edges of my father's wealth.'

'The businesses? His millions?' Christopher Trevain was white-faced.

'Ah,' the lawyer interrupted, 'I haven't quite finished. You, Christopher Trevain, may continue the fish whole-sale and retail business, but my client specifically states that you are to fund it yourself, with no more business loans from your father's estate.'

'But surely . . . is that it?' Peter Trevain stuttered.

'If you will allow me to finish . . . ' Charlie Liddicoat said.

But Patricia could keep silent no longer. She pointed to the woman in black. 'She surely isn't ... what precisely is she doing here?'

The woman stood up, tall, smartly dressed, beautifully but discreetly made-up, dark-eyed, silver-haired.

'I am Helen Thompson, from San Diego, U.S.A. I'm sorry to intrude on your family grief but I do have a part to play here, a part in which I take little pleasure but a part I faithfully promised Harry Trevain I would play.' She looked expectantly at Charlie Liddicoat who raised his eyebrows, then nodded.

'Perhaps I should finish reading the will ... ' He picked up the document. 'My ... ' that is, Sir Harry, of course ... 'final bequest, the residue of my estate, monies, properties, businesses as listed, I leave to my grandson, Ben Trevain, residing in San Diego, U.S.A., with my love and everlasting affection'.'

The silence was total. Disbelief and shock registered on all faces.

Patricia Trevain was the first to speak.

'Who — who is this Ben Trevain?

And where on earth and how on earth is he Harry's grandson?' She pointed an accusing finger at Helen Thompson. 'You! He's your grandson, isn't he? A . . . a love child!'

'Stop that,' Martha said sharply. 'Let Mr Liddicoat finish.'

'That's it, Martha, I can fill in the details . . . '

A knock on the door interrupted him as a member of the bistro staff put his head round the door.

'Sorry to interrupt but there's a visitor, says he's expected. Name of . . . um, Ben Trevain.'

★ ★ ★

A tall, broad-shouldered, dark-haired, tanned young man came into the room. 'Hi, guys, sorry I'm too late for the service but I was out of contact in South America. I flew over straight away, as soon as I heard.

'Hey, Aunt Helen.' He wrapped the woman from San Diego in a bear hug

69

which almost swung her off her feet. 'I'm sorry I missed the funeral. I guess it's all over now. But at least I get to meet the family at long last.'

'You are Sir Harry's grandson?' Peter Trevain asked, stone-faced.

'I am, though I guess Grandad's kept my existence a secret . . . '

'You're an impostor, a con man!' Peter exploded. 'How dare you come here? And how have you persuaded my father to leave you his entire fortune? I — we will fight you all the way.'

'What are you talking about?' Ben looked stunned.

'You must know — that's why you've come here, isn't it? Some charade cooked up between you and this — this woman here.'

Now Ben's dark blue eyes flashed. 'I can understand your position — you're in shock — but there's no need to insult my aunt.' Suddenly he sat down. 'What on earth — I had no idea. Aunt Helen . . . ?'

She shrugged. 'I knew he'd left you

something, but this . . . well . . . '

Martha Trevain suddenly got up and went to Ben. She lifted his chin, looked searchingly at him, frowned slightly, then smiled.

'Welcome. I've been expecting something like this for a long time.'

Peter Trevain stood up. 'There has to be a mistake,' he shouted. 'It's ridiculous. He's an impostor. We'll contest this, you just wait . . . '

'I don't think you would get very far, Peter.' Mr Liddicoat shook his head. 'As you well know, your father was a very astute man. His will is absolutely watertight.'

'Rubbish! He wasn't in his right mind! The last couple of years, he was a recluse — barmy. I . . . we'll fight it.'

The lawyer sighed. 'That is your prerogative, of course, but it'll cost you. You could lose a fortune.'

'I haven't got a fortune, blast you.' Peter glared at the young man.

'You haven't heard the last of this, whoever you are,' Jack snapped.

Ben Trevain got to his feet and put an arm round his aunt. 'I'm sure I haven't, but I assure you, this is a total shock to me, too.' As he looked around the room, his eyes stopped at Daisy, lingered, and passed on.

'I'm sorry, what more can I say? I'm as surprised as any of you. I had absolutely no idea this was Grandad's intention.'

'Well, be assured *our* intention is to fight you to the last. There is no way you, whoever you are, are getting your hands on *our* inheritance.' Peter, Jack and Christopher Trevain were, for once in their lives, united.

'Gentlemen, ladies, please.' Charlie Liddicoat rapped sharply on the table. 'This is most unseemly. Remember what today is . . .'

'We shan't forget it in a hurry.' Peter Trevain, red-faced with fury, rounded on the solicitor. 'What do you expect, what would your reaction be in the same situation? I guess you'd be combing through your law books to find a way round it. How could you let my father make such a will? He couldn't have been right in the head!'

'Peter, stop this!' Martha stood up. 'Just be quiet, all of you — respect your father's memory.'

'How can we do that?' Jack, equally furious, snapped at his mother. 'How could he be so unfair? What have we done to deserve this?'

'It's probably what you *haven't* done, Jack,' Martha answered tartly. 'You've hardly been to see him these last ten years. You've roamed about the world with barely a glance back to either of us. So I might ask you the same question — what have we, Harry and I, done to deserve such neglect? And Daisy, too — she's never had a proper father . . . '

'Oh, don't, Granny, please,' Daisy said, 'it isn't helping, and I've told you over and over, you and Grandad have been more to me than any parents. Sorry, Dad.' She turned to her father. 'I don't think you have a right to blame

Grandad; inheritance shouldn't be an automatic right, you have to earn it.'

'And you have, I suppose,' Peter Trevain snapped. 'Miss Goody Two-Shoes, apple of her grandfather's eye, of course.'

'That's not fair.' Guy Trevain leapt to Daisy's defence.

'And you're just as bad, from what I hear.' Jack turned on his nephew. 'Wheedling your way into his good books, model student, holiday jobs in Harry's businesses . . . '

'We'll fight this anyway,' Peter Trevain interrupted, glaring at the solicitor.

'As I said before, you can try, but it won't get you very far. Harry Trevain made this will over a year ago. Dr Ross, I believe, guaranteed Harry's mental condition — he was certainly in his right mind.'

'And how do we know this . . . ' Peter pointed to Ben Trevain ' . . . this person is truly Harry Trevain's grandson?'

'Because Harry Trevain said so,' the lawyer replied somewhat wearily. 'I'm going to leave you now to cool down and make what you can of the situation. Martha, I have a personal letter for you from Harry, written at the same time as the will.' He handed her an envelope. 'I was assured the contents are entirely personal and I was asked to . . . er . . . ' He looked round the room, embarrassed and perturbed by the hostile, scowling faces. Patricia Trevain's look of malevolent hatred was directed at him and the woman standing behind him, Helen Thompson.

'And, Martha, I was to assure you of his love and devotion throughout his life. I promised faithfully I would do that.'

'Rubbish!' Peter Trevain snapped. 'How could he do that at the same time as making paupers out of her sons?'

'That is not my domain.' The lawyer shut his briefcase and turned to Martha, who was clutching Harry's envelope to her heart. She looked calmly at her angry sons.

'You are hardly paupers. Your father

has supported you throughout your lives. Perhaps that's where we . . . he, went wrong. Peter, you were director of two of his companies, both of which went bankrupt.'

'That wasn't my fault, it was . . . '

Martha shook her head. 'I don't want to hear it. Harry gave you many chances, so there's no point in being angry now.'

'You bet there is. We aren't going to let this go. I'll be seeing my lawyer tomorrow. Jack, Christopher, are you with me?'

'I've nothing to lose,' Jack grunted.

'I'm . . . I'm not sure.' Christopher looked worried. 'At least I keep the fish business and things are looking up a bit there. Of course, I could do with a lot more capital . . . '

'You fool!' his wife hissed. 'We can't possibly manage on what that business brings in. We need cash . . . '

'Ma,' Guy put an arm round his mother's shoulder, 'don't worry, there's loads of potential in Trevain Fisheries.

Grandad and I often spoke about it.'

'You did?' His father frowned. 'That's the first I've heard of it. George, did he confide in you?'

'No. I hardly ever saw him. He was locked away for over a year . . . '

'He wasn't 'locked away',' Daisy said hotly. 'He was perfectly free to come and go, but he didn't want to leave his flat here, and you never made the slightest move to come and see him.'

'Fair enough, I suppose.' George was philosophical. 'I guess it's my brother Guy who has the golden touch.'

'I liked talking to him,' Guy protested.

Helen Thompson stepped forward. 'I've had enough. I'm sorry but I can't bear any more of this squabbling.' She looked at her watch. 'Ben, there's a connecting flight from Newquay Airport to Heathrow in a couple of hours — I'd like to catch it if you'd run me to the airport.'

'Can't you stay on a bit, Aunt Helen?' Ben looked alarmed by the news that his only apparent ally was decamping.

'No, I must get back. I've done what Harry wanted and it's really up to you now.'

The hostility in the room was palpable until Martha went to Helen and took her hand.

'I'd like you to stay. There are so many questions ... You'd be very welcome to stay here at the Hall with me.'

'That's kind, but really I have to go back. My husband ... '

'I'm sure Uncle Barrie could manage for a day or two,' Ben said.

'No, I must leave and I'd like to catch that flight, Ben. Lady Trevain, I think you'll find the answer to some of your questions in that letter of your husband's. I — if I may, and depending on how you feel after reading Harry's letter, I'd like to visit you again sometime with my husband.'

Martha looked at her curiously. 'Of course — you would be very welcome.

But tell me just the one thing. Were you . . . were you my husband's . . . ?'

'No!' Helen cut in sharply. 'No, I knew Harry very well, he spent a lot of time in California, but I wasn't his lover. Please . . . ' She was on the verge of tears. 'This is so hard. I have to go.' Impulsively she put her arms round Martha. 'I'm so sorry about Harry. I will see you again soon. Please, Ben, let's go now.' Without looking at the still grumbling Trevains, Helen Thompson and Ben Trevain left the room.

Martha surveyed the grim faces of those left.

'I'm ashamed of you! Just calm down, all of you, and you must accept the situation.'

'But, Mother, how can you condone this weird will? What proof have we that this Ben person has anything to do with our father?' Jack, in despair, sat with his head in his hands.

Martha looked to Charlie Liddicoat.

'I'm sorry,' the solicitor replied, 'but I can only repeat that the will is perfectly valid. Your father took great care to make his wishes absolutely watertight. The will is dated a couple of years ago, before he went into retreat at Trevain Hall, and even then he was careful to keep a check on his global interests. He had some good managers, and his assets are considerable in spite of some business failures, and he has left it all to Ben Trevain, either to dispose of, or to keep the companies viable as he thinks fit.'

'We're ruined.' Jack Trevain, pale and haggard, suddenly looked like an old man and Daisy's heart went out to him.

'Dad, don't worry. We'll manage. Stay here for a while, stop wandering round the world. Get . . . er, Jude to join you here. Come home.'

'That's sensible advice,' Charlie Liddicoat observed as he picked up his briefcase. 'Now, I must go and let you recover your composure. If you want me I'll be in my office. Martha, we'll meet soon.'

At the door he paused and looked

around at the Trevain faces, still in shock.

'I'm sorry you have taken this so badly, but I have to say that Sir Harry, and wealthy men like him, have a right to dispose of their assets in any way they see fit, and I know my client was acting in the best interests of his family. Martha dear, ring me soon.'

'I will. Thank you, Charlie. I'll see you out.'

★ ★ ★

Once Martha and Charlie had left the room, bedlam threatened once more and it was Patricia Trevain who eventually took charge.

'Will you all stop talking at once? What we need here is some organisation. We must have a plan, and we must work together to stop this ridiculous situation of all our . . . *your* Trevain money going overseas to a perfect stranger who is almost certainly an impostor.'

'Mum,' Guy said, 'it's clear this Ben Trevain is no impostor. We have to take the solicitor's word for that, and if those are Grandad's wishes I'm not going to join in a fight.'

'That's all well and good for you,' snapped Peter. 'He's paved your way in gold and you've no family to support.'

'What's that got to do with it?' Daisy said. 'Nobody has the *right* to inherit.'

'It's family money.' Her father, Jack, was ashen-faced and his hands trembled as he poured himself more whisky. Peter held out his own glass for a refill, then both sat down away from the rest of them.

'It's done for me,' Jack muttered. 'Jude will be off like a hare once she knows there's no inheritance.'

'Shame on her,' Peter was sympathetic. 'What's she like?'

'Young, beautiful, greedy for money, and she doesn't 'do' families.'

'We'll have to put a stop to this nonsense then.' Peter sipped his whisky thoughtfully. 'Tell you what, let's you and I lie low for a bit, play possum, let the rumpus die down, make a plan . . . '

'What about Chris?'

'Chris is really a free agent. We'd have to deal with Patricia, too, and there's something at the fish market, something going on . . . Let's keep it between ourselves for a bit . . . Ah, Daisy . . . ' With an effort he put a smile on his face. 'Congratulations, you've done well for yourself.'

'What?' Daisy had been prepared to placate her father and her uncle and was deflated by their apparent calm.

'The bistro — doing well, by all accounts. I haven't been yet, so I . . . '

'You must. I'll book you a table for next week. It's shameful that you haven't seen your niece in action. You too, Dad, you and Jude. You are staying on a bit to help Grandma, aren't you?'

'Of course he is,' Peter said swiftly. 'We're all going to sort this out together. Call . . . er, Jude, is it? Invite her round.'

Peter reached for the whisky bottle

and splashed some of the golden liquid into his empty glass.

'I hope you're not driving home,' Guy said, frowning.

'No, no, I'll crash here, there'll be a bed for me somewhere.'

Daisy and Guy exchanged glances.

'I'll make coffee,' Daisy said. 'Molly and Sam have gone home.' But she hesitated, looking doubtfully at her father. 'So you've come round to accepting Grandad's will, then?'

'Well,' Peter nudged his brother, 'there's not much we can do, Jack, is there, if that's what the old man wanted. Who are we to interfere? Coffee would be great, Daisy. Come on, Jack, let's have a word with Christopher and Mrs Regimental-Sergeant-Major Patricia. Off you go, children — you too, George. See you later.'

* * *

'Well, well.' Outside in the hall with Guy and Daisy, George looked puzzled.

'Was all that fire and brimstone earlier all hot air then?'

'Don't you believe it,' Guy said. 'They're up to something. We need to keep an eye on them. Coming to help make coffee, George?'

'Nah, got a date. Catch you later.'

'OK. George, you don't seem too put out by the will,' Guy observed.

George shrugged. 'I did get five thousand, and I don't believe in inherited money anyway.'

'So you'll redistribute your bit to the poor and needy?' Guy teased.

'Not on your life! Neither will Daisy open up the bistro to the county's down-and-outs, will you, Daisy?'

'Probably not — I need to make a living.'

'Fair enough. I'll tell you what, though — we need to keep an eye on the oldies. I don't believe for a second that they're going to accept this will. I feel sorry for Ben Trevain, too — he looked a decent enough guy. Harry's a sly one, isn't he, leading a double life all these years.'

'We don't know that,' Daisy protested hotly. 'Ben may very well be an impostor.'

'Come on, Daisy.' Guy laughed. 'George is right, Harry was an old dark horse . . .'

'If you're going to talk like that about my grandad . . .'

'OK, OK, sorry,' Guy apologised. 'You go off on your date, George, I'll stay here with Daisy. Once Gran's read her letter . . .'

'She'll not say anything yet, if at all, but thanks, Guy, I'd appreciate your company.'

'Right, I'll put the kettle on, sober up the seniors.'

★ ★ ★

At busy Newquay Airport 'quite decent guy' Ben Trevain shepherded his aunt Helen to a quiet corner.

'You look terrible, Aunt Helen. Just sit and I'll get you a cup of coffee — or

86

a glass of wine?'

'I think wine would be more effective. I feel quite shell-shocked. What a dreadful day! Those Trevains — no wonder Harry wanted to spend so much time with us in the States.'

'That's a bit hard, Aunt. Grandad was always torn. But his wife, Martha, she seems real nice.' He glanced up at an information board. 'Looks we've got a half hour. I'll get you a drink.'

'Thanks, Ben, you're a dear.'

Left to herself Helen Thompson closed her eyes and sighed. It had been far worse than she'd expected. Harry leaving most of his fortune to Ben — it was a great shock; she'd never for a moment dreamed he'd do that. A small legacy, maybe, but . . . but Harry had loved Ben right from the start, idolised him even — but this? She didn't know what to do. She should have made Barrie come with her; he'd have known what to do.

On impulse she pulled out her mobile to text him, and halfway through the message Ben came back with wine and coffee.

'Here you are. It's the best I could find. Hey, are you messaging Uncle Barrie? Here, let me add my bit . . . '

'No!' She snatched the phone back.

'Sorry. I didn't mean — is it kinda personal?'

'Yes.' She tried to smile. 'Personal, for his eyes alone.'

Ben smiled indulgently. 'You two are a great couple, Aunt Helen. I'll miss my visits to you, but I guess I'll have to stay in England for a while.'

'Yes, I think you will, dear.' She took a large gulp of wine and exhaled slowly, trying to calm herself. Barrie will know what to do, she told herself, reaching out to take Ben's hand.

'Ben dear, you know you're like a son to us, always have been. Well, this money, I don't . . . '

'Aunt Helen, the more I think about it, the more plans I have for it. There are so many causes, so much good to do — and Grandad trusted me to do it.

I'm proud of that. I guess I'll have to square it with the family somehow — get them to help, maybe. I'll go right back to Trevain Hall once your plane's gone.'

'Ben, I have to . . . '

But he had just spotted a new announcement on the board.

'Look, Aunt Helen, your flight is almost boarding. We have to say goodbye for a while. Maybe I can persuade the young Trevains to visit California. They were pretty angry today, but I can work on that. I have to, for Grandad Harry's sake.

'Oh, Ben . . . '

'Bye, Aunt Helen.' He hugged her. 'Give my love to Barrie — it seems an age since I last saw him. There's so much to tell you both — Peru . . . and now this. Call me from London.'

He watched his aunt through Security until he lost sight of her, then he turned to walk back to the car park, his head buzzing with plans. He couldn't wait to get back to Pencreek to get to know his Cornish relatives.

A New Awareness

★ ★ ★

As Ben Trevain drove back towards Pencreek he tried to come to terms with the startling news of his legacy. Harry Trevain's visits to California had been very regular, six or seven times a year at least. Ben had looked forward to his visits, and the two of them had developed a special relationship. Ben had wanted to visit England and particularly Cornwall, but Harry had constantly evaded the issue. 'The time isn't right,' or, 'My other family — I have to prepare them,' he had said, and Ben had had to accept that.

As Ben had begun to grow from boy to man he and Harry had found shared interests. Ben's career as a documentary filmmaker had both delighted and intrigued his grandfather. Harry had already put money into the small company Ben worked for, and he'd greatly admired Ben's reports on world poverty.

At the crossroads to Pencreek Ben hesitated, then decided he would take the road to Trevain Hall before checking into the hotel his aunt had booked for him. It was only just dusk and he reckoned his first duty was to the Trevain family.

There were lights on at the Hall and a couple of cars still in the courtyard. He parked his hire car and rang the bell.

'Oh, it's you.' Daisy opened the door wider.

'Hi, is it too late for a visit? I'll go away if it is but I thought . . . '

'No, it's not too late, but we didn't expect . . . There's only Granny and my cousin, Guy — the others have left.'

'I can go away, come back in the morning.'

'No, you may as well come in. We have to get to know each other. Come in, there's food and wine.'

'Maybe food — and coffee would be

good. I'm driving back to town, but I thought . . . well, we ought to talk.

'Yes.' Daisy looked more closely as he stepped into the hall: tall, broad-shouldered, and dark blue eyes that returned her look with interest. She could see no trace of her grandfather, Harry, in Ben Trevain's looks.

'Er, come through to the sitting-room, Granny and Guy are there. I'll get you some food.' She opened the sitting-room door. 'It's Ben Trevain,' she announced.

'Hi,' he stood awkwardly in the doorway.

Martha came forward and took his hand. 'Ben, I'm glad you came back. Did your aunt catch her plane?'

'Yes, thank you.' Another pause. 'Look, Lady Trevain, and Guy, isn't it? I'm sorry. This must have been a terrible shock to you all. I can only repeat what I said before — that it's a shock to me, too. But I think we have to deal with it before I can decide what I should do.'

'You're right, dear,' Martha said. 'Do sit down and tell us about yourself. I assume you knew about us, but we didn't have the faintest idea you existed.'

Ben took a seat opposite Martha.

'So it must have been a terrible shock for you all, I can see that. But Grandad told me about you. He told me had another family in the United Kingdom and later he talked about Cornwall a lot.'

'Didn't you think it a bit odd?' Guy asked.

'No, I didn't. I guess kids just accept what they're told. I used to look forward so much to Grandad's visits. He always brought me terrific toys, a kid's dream really. I . . . ' He broke off as Daisy came in with a tray of food which she put on a small side table next to his chair.

'Here you are, pasties and salad. OK?'

'Fine. That's something else Grandad told me about — Cornish pasties. He tried to buy them in California but never had much success!'

'These are the genuine thing, made in the bistro by my chef, Martin.'

'He spoke about the bistro, too. He was so proud of you, Daisy.'

'Good.' Daisy busied herself pouring coffee for everyone, casting covert glances at Ben as she did so. His presence filled the room as he began to relax. He was attractive, easy to like. She looked for signs of Trevain kinship but he had none of the family characteristics. Maybe he was too American, or maybe when they knew him better, because that was what they would have to do, get to know this guy who had captivated her grandad to such an extent that he had left him the bulk of the family fortune.

'So, do you live in San Diego?' Guy asked, doing his own mental analysis of the stranger.

'I did, but during the past few years I've been a bit of a nomad. My work takes me all over the world.'

94

'What's that? Your work?' Guy took his cup of coffee from Daisy.

'I make documentary films.'

'Interesting. Are you freelance?'

'No, I work for a company, but now — well, things may change.'

'I suppose they're bound to. So what . . . ?'

'So tell us about your family,' Martha interrupted swiftly. 'Your . . . mother? She swallowed; it was difficult to ask the questions nearest to her heart and she hadn't yet had the courage to read her husband's letter.

'Well, my father, Percy . . . '

'Trevain?' Martha asked.

'Yes, that was his name. I hardly knew him. He was an explorer. He and my mother died in Africa when I was only two years old — they drowned in a freak monsoon. I know very little about them. Aunt Helen and Uncle Barrie brought me up.'

'Your aunt?' Martha looked puzzled.

'Yes. I know this sounds odd but they, and Grandad, of course, are

95

— *were* — my only family. That's how it was and I never questioned it. It was a good, happy childhood. Helen and Barrie were to all intents and purposes my mum and dad, and Harry Trevain was my Father Christmas and lovely grandad all rolled into one.'

Martha had her head down to hide her tears. 'And . . . Percy's mother, your grandmother — she was Harry's . . . ?'

Ben put aside his plate and went to sit by Martha, taking her hand.

'This must be so painful; I didn't realise the full significance for you. I'm really, really sorry. I should never have come here. This legacy will surely be a burden, it's upset you all. I can't . . . '

'No, no, please, Ben, don't blame yourself. You see, Harry spent so much of his time in the States that I began to suspect . . . I fear your grandad lived a double life, which was bound to come out when he left you his fortune.'

'If I can use it wisely . . . '

'That's a different matter. Right now I'm trying to understand . . . your granny, Percy's mother . . . ?'

'I never knew her. She died just after my dad was born. Aunt Helen — well, she's my great aunt, I suppose, since she's Percy's mother's younger sister. She brought up my dad, then he married Olga, they had me, and then Helen and Barrie adopted me when my parents were killed in Africa.'

'So you never knew Percy's mother?'

'No, she was never spoken of. I'm sorry I can't be more helpful. I have no memory except of Helen and Barrie Thompson, and Harry Trevain, of course. Perhaps your letter, Lady Trevain . . . ?'

'Maybe, but this is enough for the moment. I'm quite tired, so if you don't mind . . . ?'

'I should go,' Ben said quickly.

'No, no. Where are you staying? We have plenty of room here.'

'The Dragon, in town. Aunt Helen booked me a room.'

'There's room here,' Martha repeated.

'Thank you very much, it's kind of

you, but I think it's too early. There's too much to take in. I need to get to know you all.'

'That's for sure,' Guy put in.

'I have one request before I go.' Martha looked weary, drained, and for the first time Daisy saw her granny as an old woman. 'Daisy, dear, it's asking a lot but . . . you couldn't take a few days off, could you?'

'I've already arranged to take time off from the bistro, though I'll keep an eye on things. Why?'

'Well, it would be a great kindness to Ben and a relief for me if you would look after him for a day or two — show him the village, be seen around with him.'

'Why, Gran?' Guy asked.

'Because I . . . we must accept him as Harry's heir and the village must accept that *we* accept him and welcome him into our lives. I do for Harry's sake, and I hope you do as well — both of you.'

'But isn't it a bit . . . um . . . early?'

Daisy had mixed feelings about spending time with Ben. He was very attractive, and it was hard having to accept him as family, nor did she relish parading him around Pencreek.

'Shouldn't Ben have his own space for a while? When do you have to go back to America?' she asked him.

'My time's my own. I've had a hard six months in Peru but that's done now. I'm between assignments and I *want* to be here. It's Grandfather's home. He loved it, and I want to love it, too. So please, Daisy . . . '

'Couldn't you do it, Guy? I really should be at the bistro.'

'You just said . . . '

'For goodness' sake don't argue about it!' Ben put his hands to his ears. 'I've caused enough trouble already. I'll find my own way around.'

'I'm sorry,' Daisy capitulated. 'I didn't mean to be rude, it's just . . . '

'A bit sudden?' Ben smiled at her. 'For me, too.'

She smiled back. 'It'll be fun.'

'Good.' Martha looked relieved. 'Thank you, Daisy. There will be lots of gossip, of course, but if we acknowledge Ben as Harry's grandson and heir that's all anyone needs to know.'

'There'll be a lot of guess work and wild theories,' Guy said. 'I expect I can find a bit of time, too, next week, to show you around, Ben — after my exams. I'm off to the States in the autumn anyway — work placement for a year.

'And I'm taking Granny on a trip as well so we can all meet up,' Daisy announced.

'Sounds good. Aunt Helen would love to welcome you to San Diego.'

'It's early days.' Guy stretched and yawned. 'I'm off now, to see what Mum and Dad are plotting.' He got up and shook hands with Ben. 'It's good to meet you, and good luck. You'll be fine with Daisy, she knows everyone for miles around.'

'But I think we'll start somewhere other than in the village,' she suggested.

'We'll let the news filter out for a while. If the weather's good we could take a picnic to the north coast. You'll come, Gran?'

'No. I think a day or two's rest and relaxation is what I need. It's been a trying time and I need to be quiet and on my own to ready Harry's letter. I'll join you later in the week, maybe, and you need to pay a visit to Charlie Liddicoat, Ben. There's a mass of stuff to go through.' She reached up to kiss him on the cheek and he put his arms round her.

'Thank you, Lady Trevain, you've been wonderful.'

'Not Lady Trevain, please — Martha will do.'

* * *

Next morning was bright and sunny, with clear blue skies and a light breeze. Ben had returned his hire car so Daisy picked him up at The Dragon with a picnic basket stuffed with food left over from the funeral tea. She felt relaxed and cheerful. Both she and Martha had slept well and had had an early breakfast together. She determined to forget the bistro for the day and to do her duty by her new cousin. He had brought stacks of maps and a guide-book.

'You won't need those,' she told him 'I know this county like the back of my hand.'

'Ah, but I need to know more than just the places. I need your history.'

'First things first, admire the scenery. The north coast is very different from our side of the county.'

'I like the sound of 'our county'. Does that include me?'

'It has to, since you own bits of it, or at least have fingers in several of its pies.'

'Wow! Do I really? You know, I feel real sad for Harry, but from what I can gather he was pretty tired of life. I can't thank him enough for giving me this great opportunity.' He turned to look at

Daisy. Her eyes were on the road as he said, 'I hope I can make him proud of me, Daisy.'

'I'm sure he would have been, Ben,' she replied, and meant it as she looked forward to the rest of the day with him.

That same bright morning Peter and Jack Trevain had an appointment with a firm of solicitors Peter had had dealings with before.

'They're not quite so 'stick to the rules' as the Liddicoats,' he confided to his brother. 'This is a firm of younger chaps who may have some bright new angles on the inheritance business. They helped Christopher over a bit of a sticky patch a year or two back.'

'Any use at evading debt collectors?' Jack mumbled gloomily.

'Hardly their line of business, I'm afraid, but if they can guide us in the right direction to overturn this will, you'll not be needing them. How bad is it, by the way?'

Jack whispered a figure, and even Peter, who had frequently had to be bailed out of debt by Harry, looked shocked. 'How on earth did you . . . ?'

'Don't. I know all the questions, just none of the answers.'

'So, this is serious then. We have to get the will set aside, overturned, or whatever the legal term is. And, Jack, I know we haven't been the best of friends in the past; maybe too many years between us . . . I remember when you were born and what a darned nuisance I thought you were — the household was turned upside down, Ma always busy feeding or bathing you. No wonder I couldn't stand you.'

'Thanks. I was always jealous of you, though you were some big brother, always showing off, throwing your weight around.'

'Time for a truce now, then? There's too much at stake for both of us.'

'I'm game. It'll be a nice change to be friends.' Jack brightened up a fraction. Peter had always had stacks more confidence than he had himself, Jack thought.

Maybe we can pull this off, he mused. I'd be grateful forever, out of debt, in with Jude — and maybe treatment for the gambling addiction that had brought him close to ruin. In fact, if they didn't manage to rescue the inheritance, it really would mean ruin. He shuddered.

'Friends then.'

'Sure. Friends,' Peter repeated.

Outside the lawyers' smart modern offices they shook hands and went into to keep their appointment.

★ ★ ★

On the other side of the county Daisy and Ben had walked several miles of coastal path marked by dramatic rocks jutting up from the sea. Stops were frequent as Ben paused to take in the foaming white surf sweeping onto golden sands. Black-suited surfers poised on boards eyed the waves, looking always for the ultimate ride.

'Magnificent,' he breathed as the cliff

path turned into more scenic delights. 'Just beautiful. Grandad never told me about this.'

'I thought California . . . '

'Not quite like this. Great surf, of course, but this is tremendous scenery.' He indicated the wide sweep of sea and the rocky coast.

'Grandad was a fisherman first and foremost, no time for what he called 'tourist trappings'. He loved to sail, though, and to go out with the fishing boats. Did you know he started Trevain Enterprises by catching fish and selling it on Pencreek harbour quay?'

Ben nodded. 'I did hear that one, many times. Gee, I'm starving. What about having our picnic here?' He pulled off the rucksack that Daisy had provided.

'Why not? Springy grass, marvellous sea view, and look, over there, that old tin mine in the distance — the path leads past it before we work our way back to the car park.'

'Great. Hardly anyone about, too.'

'It's early, but the season is just about to start and there'll be plenty of hikers then.'

'This is better.' Ben unrolled a waterproof mat while Daisy unpacked the food.

'It's mainly leftovers, I'm afraid. Rosie and Martin, from the bistro, catered the pre-funeral dinner and afternoon tea on the day, so now it's pasties again, I'm afraid.'

'Suits me. Hey, beer, too, and still cold! You're a genius, Daisy — this is just what I need.' He held out the bottle to her.

'I'd better not, we've quite a long drive back. There's water for me — you have the beer.'

He took a long pull before flopping back on the turf and closing his eyes.

'This is an improvement on the wilds of Peru.'

'What were you doing there?'

'Oh, ecological stuff, poverty, hardship. Now it's on to the next thing.'

'Which is?'

He sat up. 'Well, you won't believe this, but I was thinking of doing some UK work. I asked Grandad so many times if I could film here in Cornwall. It was the one thing he stood out against, absolutely adamant, and he got so upset that I just let it go in the end. I guess he wanted to keep his two families apart.'

'So he did talk about us?'

'Oh, sure. I knew you were Daisy the minute I set eyes on you.'

'That's because I'm the only girl in the pack!'

'No. No, he loved you so much, I'd get jealous when I was much younger.'

'But surely . . . didn't you think it strange — two families, two homes?'

Ben took another swig of beer.

'Not really, that's how it was and I never knew anything different. Helen and Barrie were Mom and Pop, they were my home. Grandad was like Father Christmas except that he turned up at the house more often.

'Out of your lot, you and Guy were his favourites. And his wife, Martha

— he loved her. There's another young guy — George — he quite liked. He hardly mentioned his sons, and having seen them in action, I can't blame him. Until I was properly grown up you were all part of a sort of fantasy story he made up to amuse us.'

'Oh.' An inexplicable wave of sadness hit Daisy. His 'fantasy story', 'another world'. Tears wouldn't hold back. She dropped her pastie on the grass, buried her head in her hands and sobbed.

'Hey, Daisy, I'm sorry . . . Here . . . ' He moved rapidly and took her in his arms. 'Daisy, don't cry, please. You're a happy girl, Grandad said.'

As her tears flowed and huge sobs shook her, Ben pulled her closer. 'Hush, it's all right. It's been a bad time here, I shouldn't have gone on.'

'No, I want to know, what it was like . . . ' As her tears gradually stopped she was conscious of Ben's warm skin against her cheek. When he'd taken off his shirt to enjoy the sun she'd noticed smooth brown chest muscles. His hands were stroking her shoulders, soothing her as if she was a child.

For a few seconds she lay there, comforted by his warmth and strength — it was a good place to be. He pushed her hair back, looked into her tear-filled eyes and gently lowered his lips to her forehead. She closed her eyes, relaxed, sighed, but then a blinding flash of insight hit her. What was she thinking? It had started as a hug of comfort but was coming dangerously close to something else. Impossible.

'Sorry, sorry.' She sat up and wiped her eyes. 'I don't know what came over me.' She took a long drink of water and tried to laugh. 'Sorry,' she said again. 'It must have been the beer.'

'You didn't drink any.' Ben was looking at her curiously. 'You had water.'

'Oh, yes, of course. Well, the sun and the sea air . . . ' Aware that she was babbling, she turned to gather up the picnic things, trying to erase from her mind that moment and Ben's warmth against her cheek.

'Well,' she said, changing into brisk tourist guide mood, 'if you want to have a look at that mine we'd better be moving.'

'OK.' He began to roll up the mat, punching it into shape to fit his backpack, each avoiding the other's eyes. 'I'm interested in that; I've got quite a dossier on the Cornish American connection. Mining played a big part in both histories.'

'Really? Guy did something like that way back when he was doing A levels.'

Now they were moving on, striding out towards the old tin mine's skyward pointing finger, chatting as naturally as before, but neither could forget that brief moment of perfect harmony between them, nor did they want to forget it, though they could never admit it.

★　★　★

'I'm sorry, Mr Trevain, but from what you tell me I don't think there's much chance of a successful outcome if you contest your father's will.'

'No loopholes, no procedures . . . new laws?'

'We should need to see a copy of the will before we commit ourselves, and we can try if that's what you want, and, of course, it is a considerable estate, but a lengthy court battle would severely erode your capital if there was no outcome in your favour.'

'But if we prove he's not a Trevain, which I strongly suspect?'

'On what grounds?'

'Um . . . he doesn't look anything like one of the family.'

'Hardly legal grounds to contest a will,' the solicitor said dryly.

'DNA testing?'

'Not our field. And you would need his consent, of course.'

'So there's nothing you can do?'

The young lawyer looked quizzically at the brothers.

'I repeat, if you are determined on this we can set the wheels in motion, but it will be costly, and, unless the entire Trevain family is behind you, acrimonious. Is Lady Trevain in favour of this?'

Peter frowned. 'Not unless we can persuade her, which I doubt.'

'She is well provided for?'

'Of course. Our father was a devoted husband.'

'She knew of this young man from America then?'

'No.'

'She sort of suspected, apparently,' Jack interrupted.

'It's a difficult situation. I'm sorry I can't be more positive.'

'So that's it?' Peter was still frowning.

'Unless you decide to proceed, but my advice is against that course of action, though we would, of course, be pleased to act for you if you decide to contest the will.' He looked at his watch. 'If there's nothing more just now, I have another appointment . . . '

'Typical blooming lawyers,' Peter complained as he and Jack found the nearest pub for lunch. 'And I bet his bill for that piece of non advice will cost us.'

'It'll have to cost you, not me,' Jack pointed out. 'I've run out of credit practically everywhere.'

'I'll be buying lunch then?'

'Thanks, Peter. I'll pay you back, if and when.'

'Oh, forget it, I'm not that hard-up yet.' He went to the bar to order two meals and came back with refills of beer. 'Cheers.'

'Hardly, in the circumstances.' Jack stared gloomily into his pint.

'For goodness' sake, cheer up. We're not done yet.'

'So what can we do?'

'Drastic circumstances need drastic measures.'

'Meaning?'

'If there are no legal means we look for other ways.'

'For instance?'

Peter took a pull at his pint.

'Scare him off — soften him up, then scare the living daylights out of him and send him winging back to where he came from.'

'Come on, Peter, he doesn't look the type to scare easily, especially when there's a fortune at stake.'

'We can but try. It's the only way we're going to get our hands on our father's money — and I'm still convinced this bloke's an impostor.'

'We've got to prove that, of course. We could hire a private detective, maybe?'

'That's a thought. I wonder how much that would cost?'

'Mother wouldn't know, and forget the cost for now. I'll sound out Christopher — he should pay his whack.'

Their lunches arrived and they started to eat.

'Hey,' Jack said after a few minutes, 'here's a wheeze — we could always take him out in the boat and drown him, drop him over the side.'

Peter spluttered. 'We'd never get away with that!'

'I'm only kidding! It was joke! I'm not that much of a fool.'

They went back to their lunches, and silence.

★ ★ ★

Ben spent a long time around the defunct tin mine on the cliff top, taking photographs from all angles, making notes and referring to one of his guide books. Daisy leaned against a boulder and watched him, eyes half closed, almost dozing in the sunshine.

After a while Ben came to sit beside her.

'This is fascinating! It's great to be here when I've read so much about mining in this area. Did you know the miners had to tunnel a very long way out under the sea to get the tin out? Dangerous work, too.'

'Yes, I do know a bit about it.

Grandad told me lots.'

'Really? Both of us then. Daisy?' Ben shifted round to face her. 'I've decided I'm going to stay here a while. Do you think there might be a house or a cottage I could take in Pencreek?'

'Pencreek? That's a bit close.'

'Is that a problem? I need to integrate, and the best way would be to live here for a while, surely?'

'I thought we were going to do it gradually.'

'That was Lady Trevain's idea. If I'm going to be filming in the area, Pencreek would be a good base.'

'You've got plans for filming here?'

'Documentaries, yes. A whole raft of them: mining, fishing, emigration, a series, finishing off with a Cornwall-California connection.'

'Wow. This is sudden.'

'No, it's not. Through Grandad Harry I've learned so much theory and now I want to put it into practice. What's wrong, don't you approve?'

'It's not for me to approve — it's all a

bit sudden, that's all.'

'Not in my head, it isn't. Daisy, it's been there for years, through Grandad Harry — he put it all here.' He tapped his temple. 'Now I want to get it out, share it, and he's made it possible with his legacy. I'll use it in the area, try to do some good. Will you help me?'

'I don't know the slightest thing about filming.'

'You don't have to, I have my own team. But you can help, advise, show me the county, and introduce me to the people.'

'Well . . . ' It was difficult not to catch his enthusiasm. 'I suppose we could start in Pencreek this evening. I need to look in at the bistro.'

'Could we have supper there? I'd like to see it.'

'Perhaps. We'd better get back anyway. See that line of cloud out there? It's probably a storm coming in. There'll be high tides tonight — it often happens at this time of year.'

'OK. But hang on a minute.' He

picked up his camera and focused on her. 'Good background.' He pressed the button. 'Got you, Daisy Trevain.'

Ben's mood of exhilaration lasted throughout the journey back to the hotel. He talked of further projects, admired the scenery, and finally declared that it had taken him just one day to be entirely captivated by Cornwall.

'There are plenty of other places to visit,' Daisy said mildly. 'Scotland, Wales, the Lake District . . . '

'I know, but all in good time. I've enjoyed today, Daisy. Thank you.'

At the entrance to the Dragon he put a hand on her shoulder and was about to give her a polite thank you kiss when he stopped, withdrew his hand, and smiled.

'Thank you again — and this evening?'

'I'm going to the bistro now. I'll warn them.'

'Warn them? What do you mean?'

'Oh, well, news of your arrival will

already have flashed through the bush telegraph.'

'But I've only been here a day! And we've been the other side of the county all day.'

'They'll know, Ben, trust me. I'll come back for you in a couple of hours.'

'Can't I meet you at the bistro? I'm going to hire another car — the hotel manager promised to fix it up today.'

'OK. come straight to the bistro, just before we open at six o'clock. You'll have to park on the outskirts and then walk towards the harbour. You can't miss us.'

'Fine. Thanks again, Daisy, I appreciate your time.'

'What are families for but to help each other?' Though the modern-day Trevains didn't exactly illustrate that maxim!

★ ★ ★

At the Bistro Daisy spent an hour with Rosie going over business and planning for the coming season. Only when that was done did the two girls make coffee in Daisy's flat and relax before the evening opening.

'Sure you can cope on your own for a bit longer?' Daisy asked.

'Yes, quite easily. It'll be different in a week or two when the season's underway. All hands will be needed then.'

'Good coffee,' Rosie ventured after a long pause.

'Same as always. Go on, you can ask, I know you're desperate to.'

'Thank goodness! I'm bursting with curiosity. Everyone in the village is talking about it. So . . . ?'

Daisy sighed; it was inevitable and had to be faced.

'So, this guy from the States, Ben Trevain, turns up after the funeral just in time to hear that he's inherited the bulk of Grandad's fortune.'

'So it *is* true! I thought perhaps it was

some wild story.'

'Not at all. He's a nice bloke, actually, and stunned like the rest of. But he's full of ideas, and he's already in love with Cornwall. Actually he's coming here tonight for supper. Six o'clock, as soon as we open.'

Rosie sprang to her feet. 'And we're sitting calmly drinking coffee? What are you thinking, Daisy?'

'Well, supper, what else?'

'I have to see Martin — check the covers, change the wine, possibly the menu . . . '

'What for?'

'Daisy, think about it! He practically owns the place now — the mortgage, the loan, Sir Harry's money.'

'No, he doesn't. I own it. Grandad's will cancelled the debt and left me money for expansion, too. It could give us a future, Rosie.'

'That's a relief! But we still want to make a good impression. What does he do for a living?'

'He makes documentary films. He

plans to do lots in Cornwall.'

'How can you sit there drinking coffee when all this . . . all this stuff is going on?' Rosie's voice had risen to a squeak.

'Calm down, and let me finish my coffee. I'll introduce you to him when we go downstairs. You'll see he's just an ordinary guy, and as bewildered as we are. Dad and Uncle Peter nearly died of fury and jealousy, of course.'

'I bet! The whole village knows about him now, and if word gets around that he's coming here to eat tonight, we'll be packed out.'

'So don't tell anyone. We're going to the pub afterwards and that'll be the test. I expect that'll be packed out, too. You're sure you can manage tonight? I need to get back to Trevain Hall. Grandad left Granny a letter and she may read it today.'

Rosie went to the door as Martin came in.

'It's past opening time, you two, what are you doing? Daisy, there's a guy downstairs looking for you . . . American, is he?'

'Sorry, Martin, we forgot the time. We're on our way. And, yes, it's Ben Trevain, Sir Harry's grandson.'

'I'll tell the others,' and Martin was gone as suddenly as he'd appeared.

* * *

Any hope of a quiet supper was doomed. Every table was taken and there was an overflow in the bar. Everyone greeted Daisy, unaccustomed to seeing her eating in her own restaurant, and one or two hovered and smiled as if waiting to be introduced to her companion. With difficulty, she concentrated on the excellent fish supper Martin had produced.

'This is a great place, Daisy,' Ben said. 'It has a real buzz to it. Grandad Harry told me all about it and how hard you've worked.'

'I love it. Grandad had an idea of a bistro franchise — he told me about it that . . . that last night.' A shadow crossed her face. 'That night he was distressed, he had something on his mind. I think I know now what it was.'

She pushed back her chair. 'Look, this is getting ridiculous, it was a bad idea. The supper club ladies are over there and it's not even their night. It's a set-up — they'll all be at our table in a minute. Come on, Ben, we've the pub to do yet.'

'But I thought the whole idea was to introduce me to the village . . . '

'It'll be easier in the pub. Let's go.'

Outside, it was much quieter. The air was still, quite sultry, causing just a slight ripple on the water of the harbour.

'This is so picturesque,' Ben said, 'just as Grandad described it. This is the inner harbour where the boats are moored, and further on through those stone walls that look like arms is the outer harbour and the quay . . . '

' . . . where Grandad first sold his fish to the village.' Daisy laughed as she completed Ben's words.

'And the pub's over there on the other side,' he concluded.

'Right, and that's where we're heading. It'll be more sociable there, that's the real hub of the village.' She looked again at the rippling waters. 'It looks calm but there's a storm brewing, not a big one but enough to close the outer harbour. See, the chain's up already.'

Daisy paused at the door of the pub and looked through the window.

'It's very crowded, and people will want to speak to you in there. Grandad used to come here a couple of times a week when he was at home. Everyone will want to meet you. Here goes . . . '

A hubbub of sound greeted them but five seconds later there was total silence as everyone turned to stare, drinks suspended halfway to their lips.

'Hi, folks.' Daisy lifted her hand. 'I'm glad to see so many of you. It makes it easier for me to introduce a new family member. This is Ben Trevain from San Diego, California. He came over for Sir

Harry's funeral.' She swallowed. You could have heard a pin drop in the silence.

'I may as well tell you all, because you'll probably have heard rumours already — Ben is Harry Trevain's grandson and heir to much of Harry's business. He'd like to meet you all. He's staying in Cornwall for a while for that purpose.'

Then the hubbub really started! First came Bob, the landlord.

'Welcome, Ben, I'm pleased to have you here and pleased you're staying for a while.'

He was followed by the harbour master, the vicar, the captain of the darts team, the lifeboat crew — Daisy retired to a window seat to watch as Ben was surrounded by the pub's regular and irregular clientele.

After an hour or so she had had two glasses of orange juice, and was tired of waiting and anxious to get back to the Hall and her grandmother. She tried to catch Ben's eye, but he was obviously enjoying himself, as were the people around him. Edging nearer, she heard the leader of the Pencreek male voice choir effusively thanking Ben for his promised continued support.

Without any apparent effort, Ben seemed to have slid right into his grandfather's shoes. It was quite a remarkable achievement.

She finally caught his attention, and pointed to her watch, then in the direction of Trevain Hall.

'Granny,' she mouthed.

Immediately Ben broke away and came to her.

'We have to go now?'

'No, no, you stay, you're doing fine, but I'm worried about that letter Granny got and there's only Christopher and Patricia with her at the Hall. You stay here.'

'It's amazing. I can't believe it, Daisy, and I can't wait to start work. There's a fisherman over there who knows everything about Grandad's past. Jem Bunt, I think his name is. There's so much material here. Can I see you tomorrow?'

'I'll be up at the Hall for a day or two, then back here. I've a flat over the bistro.'

'I'll call you.' Impulsively Ben kissed her cheek. 'Thanks, Daisy.'

'What for? You're family, aren't you? I . . . '

'Hey, Ben, over here . . . '

She saw Jem Bunt beckoning to Ben. She also saw Jem's son Dave, not looking too happy and about to move towards her. She shook her head, miming 'got to go', and pushed her way out of the crowded pub into the night air where the storm was beginning to rumble, still out at sea but moving swiftly towards land. She could already feel the spray stinging her face.

Ben the Hero

As Daisy left the pub a clap of thunder heralded the sudden torrential downpour of a summer storm. She started to run back to the bistro where her car was parked, but as she turned against the wind to fasten her jacket she heard a commotion coming from the outer harbour: shouts, laughter, screeches, the sound of noisy children at play. She saw a group of youngsters gathered round a short flight of stone steps leading to boat moorings. Waves were crashing over the steps and the children appeared to be playing a version of 'chicken'.

A flash of lightning lit up a pair of figures going down the steps towards the thundering water. As the wave curled upwards the children shrieked and ran back up the steps, but waiting until the last possible moment.

'Hey, stop that, you idiots!' she yelled. 'It's dangerous.'

'Aw, it's fun. First one back's a chicken . . . '

Another pair ran down the steps as Daisy raced towards them.

'Stop right there!' she shouted, but they just gave her a cheery wave.

Daisy saw the wave before the children did; it reared up, foam-topped, suspended for a second, before it crashed with full force on to the steps. The children standing on the wall above the steps screamed as the wash caught them before it receded back over the steps. It left them still standing clutching each other — but there was no sign of the four who had gone down the steps.

Screams and shouts were almost drowned by the drumming rain but Daisy saw another figure running down the steps, calling out a name. But then he slipped on the wet stone and the next wave took him out of sight.

Panic broke out. 'They're in the

water! Oh, help us! Please . . . my little brother . . . '

A little girl clutched at Daisy's arm. 'Help . . . oh, please, please . . . '

A quick glance at the dark sea told Daisy she could do nothing on her own.

'Follow me as fast as you can. Run to the pub — keep close, hurry!'

Crying, terrified, they pressed around her. 'We didn't mean . . . '

'Done it lots of times. We can swim . . . lots of times . . . '

Panting, Daisy pushed open the pub door. The scene was as she'd left it, an animated buzz with Ben at the centre.

'Help, quickly! The harbour . . . ' She pushed the children in front of her. 'The outer harbour, by the steps — there are four, maybe five children in the water . . . '

'My little brother . . . ' Sobbing and wailing, a small girl ran to Jem Bunt. 'Uncle Jem, it's our Joshua, he's in the water.'

Daisy gathered the children to her as the men rushed out into the night. Bob, the landlord, was quickly at the door with torches and a powerful searchlight.

'Jon,' the harbour master called out, 'my office — ropes, lifebelts, flares. Hurry, hurry, I'll catch you up. Go on,' he passed over a bunch of keys, 'I'd slow you down. Run, now.'

Daisy glimpsed Ben's back, one of the first to move to lead the crowd of rescuers towards the harbour. She wanted to follow them but the children were clinging to her like sodden limpets. Mary, the landlady, ran for towels and blankets.

'Hot chocolate,' Mary commanded the remaining barman.

'We didn't mean anything,' a small child repeated over and over, 'it was only a game.'

'You shouldn't have been out on your own,' Mary said severely. 'You should be tucked up in bed asleep.'

'It's Friday night,' sobbed a young boy. 'We had youth club, and we always play in the harbour after the club. I shan't do it any more. Are they dead?'

he wailed, and that set the others off.

'Shush, shush,' Daisy soothed, wrapping his blanket more tightly around him, 'there are a lot of strong men gone to fetch them out.'

'I saw Josh clinging to a rope off a mooring ring,' one child said hopefully.

'That's good. And listen, the wind's died down a bit. The storm's moving on.'

Mary was still muttering. 'Stupid children, not like that in my day,' but her kind face expressed her agonised worry. 'It'll be a grim day for Pencreek if any of the little ones perish,' she muttered to Daisy.

Daisy looked at the pub's clock. It seemed as if the men had been long gone, and surely if the children were all safe they'd be back by now? The sea, even in early summer, would be freezing . . .

Just as she was preparing to think the worst, the door burst open and men carrying children came into the pub.

'All safe and sound! Bob's gone to

round up their parents,' said a member of the lifeboat crew with two of the children in his arms.

Ben Trevain had another, and Joshua Bunt clung to his Uncle Dave. Carefully they set the children down, wrapped them in towels and rugs and gave them hot drinks.

'Two of 'em got to the harbour steps and clung on for dear life to a boat. Josh here hung on to a rope. Little Em was harder to find and we thought she was lost at one point.' Dave Bunt shook his head and accepted a large hot whisky toddy from Mary.

'We'll need more than a chain across the entrance in future,' the harbour master said grimly.

'We won't do it again. Honest,' Josh piped up.

'Maybe not, but there's others like you just as daft. We've been lucky tonight. What might have happened — well, it doesn't bear thinking about.' He took a couple of whiskies from Mary and handed one to Ben. 'I say three cheers to our newcomer to Pencreek. I never saw a man work so hard or move so fast — dived straight in, and a great swimmer. You're the hero of the hour, Mr Trevain.'

'Please,' Ben looked horribly embarrassed, 'I was glad to help.'

'Well,' the vicar added his voice, 'we all welcome you to Pencreek. Like grandfather, like grandson — and long may you stay with us in Cornwall. Cheers.'

At that point, much to Ben's thankfulness, the children's distraught parents rushed into the pub and clutched their offspring, not knowing whether to scold or kiss but generally settling for the latter.

'Well done, Ben,' Daisy said quietly. 'But I should get some dry clothes from somewhere before you catch pneumonia.'

'I'm all right. Mary's finding me a jersey and a pair of her son's trousers. It's lucky you went out when you did, Daisy, otherwise . . . I hate to think what might have happened.'

'Well, you're certainly one of us now. You've proved yourself a true Trevain. You won't be able to put a foot wrong — ever!'

'I'm not sure about that. I'm used to these situations, that's all. The trick is not to panic. If you panic, you're lost. I've learned that so many times in far worse places than Pencreek harbour.'

'But the children . . . ?'

'It could have been much worse. They didn't panic — they just used their heads and swam for the steps and waited to be rescued. That was resourceful — it'll make a good film.'

'Ben! How could you? It could have been a tragedy!'

'Sorry, just thinking ahead. My film crew arrive in a couple of days and I've a lot to do before then.'

'Oh. Already? You're not wasting any time.'

'I'm excited, Daisy. It's not just tonight, but the spirit of the men and the kids is remarkable. In a different sort of way it's a bit like when you're stuck in some wild mountain place, or in the jungle hiding from rebel armies, or . . . '

'You've done all that?'

'Yep.' He was rubbing his hair with one of Mary's towels.

'I should keep that secret, if I were you,' Daisy advised. 'You're perfect fodder for the Ladies Supper Club, the Church Guild, the WI . . . the Allotment Association . . . '

Ben held up his hand. 'Stop, stop! Let me settle in first!'

As his hair dried it curled around his head and at the nape of his neck and she couldn't help staring. He stopped towelling.

'What? Why are you looking at me like that?'

'Sorry.' She looked away quickly. She was so intensely aware of him.

He laughed. 'I know, my hair's too long, but I didn't have time . . . no barbers in the jungle.'

'I didn't mean . . . ' She blushed, but

she was saved from trying to explain as the children were being shepherded out of the pub and they all wanted to say goodbye before they were whisked off home.

'Thanks, Daisy, and we won't play that game again.'

'Promise?'

'Er, well, not in a storm anyway.' Ever resilient, excited now that the drama was over and pleased to be the centre of attention, they trooped out, their parents holding them very firmly.

'Can I give you a lift back to your hotel, Ben?' Daisy asked.

He shook his head. 'I'll stay here until closing time. Mary's drying my clothes and there's a lot to talk about with the guys here. I'll call a taxi.'

'Fine. I'm going back to the Hall now, but I'll maybe see you tomorrow. I'll be at the bistro later in the day.'

'Catch you there, then. Goodnight, Daisy.'

Daisy left reluctantly. Ben was already the centre of attention, jotting down notes as the men spoke. He looked as though he'd been a fixture in their midst all his life.

* * *

The storm had subsided to a grey drizzle by the time Daisy reached Trevain Hall. She was surprised to see so many lights on although it was quite late. Fearing something else dramatic had happened, she ran inside, worried, perhaps, that Martha had been taken ill.

'Hello?' she called as she crossed the hall.

A murmur of voices came from the nearby small sitting-room.

'Hello?' she called again.

'In here,' Martha's voice answered without a hint of worry, and Daisy breathed a sigh of relief.

To her amazement the scene in the sitting-room was harmonious and peaceful. Her father was playing chess with her Uncle Peter as though they were bosom buddies, while Christopher and Patricia were sitting on the sofa with Martha, all immersed in gardening books. Even her cousin George, not one for visiting Trevain Hall if he could help it, was lounging in a chair with half an eye on the TV in the corner.

'Daisy,' Patricia looked up from the gardening books, 'where have you been? Martha was quite worried. Did the storm hold you up?'

'Sort of. There was an incident.' Briefly she told them about the near disaster in the harbour.

'Sounds quite dreadful,' Martha said. 'I'm glad everyone's safe.'

'Thanks a lot to Ben. Apparently he was the hero of the hour,' Daisy said.

Jack and Peter exchanged glances.

'Where is he now?' Jack asked.

'He's still at the pub, drying out.'

'What's he doing there?' Peter asked casually. 'I'd have thought he'd want to be here with his . . . er, family.'

'Why? You didn't exactly give him a warm welcome when he arrived,' Daisy retorted, 'just the opposite. No wonder he's avoiding you. Anyway, he's a great success in Pencreek now after all the drama. You should have been at the pub. Oh, and we had supper at the bistro before, and everyone wanted to take a look at the new heir.' There was a pause, long enough for Daisy to regret her enthusiasm in the circumstances.

'Try to understand our position,' her Uncle Peter said quietly, but there was an edge to his voice. 'It was a shock, seeing our inheritance pass to a stranger — an impostor claiming to be a Trevain. A betrayal, wouldn't you agree? And we're not taking it . . . ' But a nudge from Jack reminded him not to show his bitter anger.

'Er . . . there's a lot at stake,' he ended lamely.

Jack diverted attention back to Daisy. 'So, tell us about Ben Trevain. You spent all day with him yesterday — is he a genuine Trevain?'

'He's a nice enough guy, and he'll use the money well. He and Grandad were obviously close and had a real bond between them . . . '

'More than with his own sons?' Peter said bitterly. 'He hardly spent any time with us. How could he lead such a double life?' He glanced at his mother. 'It's baffling how you could not know, Ma. Did you never suspect this other family in America?'

Martha shook her head, near to tears.

'Uncle Peter,' Daisy broke in, 'don't be so bitter. You can't change things.'

'What does he do for a living?' Jack said hurriedly with a warning frown for his brother.

'He's a film maker. He makes documentaries about poverty, exploitation, global warming, that kind of thing. There's a film crew coming in a few days.'

'A film crew? Here? In Pencreek? What for?' Christopher crossed to a side table. 'Drink, anyone?'

Jack and Peter both nodded. 'Drown our disappointments. Patricia?'

'Please — and I'm not giving up even

if you are. Christopher and I have an appointment in the morning to see a lawyer, a friend of a friend . . . '

'What?' Christopher nearly dropped his glass. 'You didn't tell me.'

'That's because I knew what you would say. You're just too lazy, and we can't afford . . . '

'Cancel it. I'm still working — I haven't the time.'

'You're the boss — take time off . . . '

'I can't.' He downed his drink in one. 'You've no business . . . I have to be at the fish market tomorrow, and it's very important, so cancel it.'

'Don't worry, save your money,' Peter said acidly. 'Jack and I have already been down that route and it's no go, unless you're prepared to spend the fortune we haven't got. We can't afford that luxury, even if you can.'

Daisy sighed. So it was back to family form, with arguments, tempers and frayed nerves. So much for harmony!

Suddenly her mind blanked, then, like a computer, displayed a screen image to jog her memory. Grandfather, pleading, extracting her promise: 'set it right', 'a team', 'harmony'. Sir Harry had been asking for help, and for Ben, presumably, to be part of the Trevain family, a team working together in harmony. She looked round the sitting-room. It seemed like mission impossible.

Tension was increasing and her father and Uncle Peter were already building up a head of steam against 'the impostor'. Patricia and Christopher were also bristling with angry hostility and, with one last ferocious glare at her husband, Patricia left the room. George, with an agonised shrug towards Daisy, slid out behind her.

There was an embarrassed silence.

'Sorry, Mother,' Christopher said. 'Er . . . the stress and strain, money worries — you know.'

'Patricia said she would help me re-plan the garden, it's terribly neglected. Harry lost all interest. It'll give me something to do.'

'You're surely not planning to stay here?' Peter said. 'It's far too big for you. You'd get a good price with its building potential for retirement flats or holiday homes. I'd do it myself if I had the capital.'

'I hadn't thought,' Martha said sadly. 'I love it here and we were happy. It holds so many memories of my life with Harry, and I'd hate to leave the village.'

'Have you read his letter yet?' Daisy asked gently.

'No. No, I can't. I nearly tore it up. I'm scared . . . '

'Gran.' Daisy went to sit beside her. 'Leave it a while, it's too soon.'

'I think you should read it.' Jack was concerned. 'It might give us an idea about this Ben Trevain. You owe it to us, Mother.'

'Dad!' Daisy protested. 'It's not up to us, and it's not going to alter anything.'

Christopher got up. 'I'm going after Patricia. I've enough problems of my own without worrying about Ben Trevain. As Daisy said, we can't change anything. I'm sorry,' he said, kissing his mother's cheek. 'I hope you don't leave yet. After all, where would Pat and I live?'

'I won't make any decisions yet, Christopher. You mustn't worry.'

'Goodnight then. I'll look in tomorrow.'

'You need that holiday,' Daisy said to Martha when Christopher had gone, 'but I'm tied up until the end of the season. Dad, why don't you take Gran for a little break right now?'

He looked startled. 'Me? Well . . . there's Jude, you see.'

'No, I don't see. Where is she? Doesn't she want to meet your mother and your daughter?'

'Well, it's . . . er, difficult. She's in Spain right now — she has a friend with a villa.'

'That's ideal! That would be so good for Gran, some real sunshine . . . '

'Oh, I don't think . . . ' Martha looked alarmed.

'It's . . . um, mainly young people,

the villa party,' Jack mumbled.

'Well, that counts you out, Dad, so you can easily take Gran for a few days' break somewhere else.'

'No, I've got to go to Spain. In fact, I've booked a flight for tomorrow night. I'll be back, but I must see Jude. You don't understand.'

'I think I do,' Peter said. 'You'll go and tell her the news, and then I expect you'll be back within an hour on a return flight home.'

'Why's that?' Daisy asked.

'Oh, just a hunch. From what your dad told me earlier, as I see it — no cash, no Jude. Finished.'

'Hey, that was in confidence!' Jack protested.

'Sorry, but you'd best face it. Don't waste your money on the plane fare; phone her and break the bad news.'

'Thanks for the advice, but I'm catching an early-morning flight. So I'll say goodnight.' He glared at his older brother. 'I don't know why I confided in you. You were no help to me when I was a kid and you're no help to me now. Goodnight.'

'Well, so much for family harmony,' Daisy said after the door slammed one more time. 'Sorry, Gran. Would you like a drink of something — cocoa, maybe, or hot chocolate?'

'Actually I think I'll have a glass of wine, dear. Will you join me?'

'OK, let's have a nightcap. Uncle Peter?'

'No, thanks, I'd better make a move, too. I've a long day tomorrow — a golf tournament, though it's probably a bit pointless now since I won't be able to afford the subscription next year.'

'Don't talk such rubbish,' Martha said, 'you're not that hard-up, are you? I'll pay it if you are.'

'Would you? That would be great.'

'Uncle Peter!' Daisy gave an exasperated sigh, and Martha laughed.

'It's all right, Daisy, I'm happy to help out, but you must try to organise your finances better, Peter. You always were hopeless. You always spent your pocket money within five minutes of getting it, then wheedled Jack's out of him.'

'Did I? I don't remember that. I'm sorry, Ma, I know we're a big disappointment to you, as we were to Dad. It was Zoe who used to do the household accounts,' he said, referring to his late wife. 'Never a penny out.' He shrugged. 'After she died, I was lost. Still am, I suppose. I never did have a head for business either, much to Dad's disappointment.'

'But we both always loved you, Peter.'

'I know you did, Ma, but Dad never took much notice of us. He was too busy making his millions.' Peter's tone was laced with anger and frustration. 'You'd have thought he'd have had the decency to leave his own sons some of the wealth he neglected us to make. Why? That's what I keep asking — why did he leave his entire estate to this so-called Ben Trevain? Ma, I'm sorry, I'm going before I say worse things, and you don't deserve that. But mark my words, you'll regret being taken in, because as sure as I'm standing here that guy is an impostor, however much he's charmed the village and Daisy.'

For a brief second, to Daisy's horror, the thought slid into her heart, 'I hope he is an impostor, then it would mean that he's not my cousin.' And that would mean she was free to indulge this attraction to him . . .

With a catch of her breath she pushed the thought firmly away. Of course he wasn't an impostor. How could he be when he had talked so knowingly and lovingly of their grandfather, Harry Trevain?

Growing Into the Family

The folk of Pencreek truly mourned Sir Harry Trevain's death, but after the funeral life inevitably went on and interest switched to the new heir. Extensive coverage of the dramatic night in the harbour was the main feature in the local Press, to be echoed nationally as it coincided with Sir Harry Trevain's obituary.

When Ben moved into a tiny fisherman's cottage overlooking Pencreek harbour his place in the community was assured.

Further excitement was generated when news spread that he was 'something in films' and that a film crew was coming to Pencreek from California. The hopes of the local drama group were high until it heard that the films were documentaries, but then rose again when rumours spread that at least the films were to be Cornwall associated.

The tourist season was about to move towards its peak summer period: restaurants, hotels, rock shops and ice cream parlours were dusted down refurbished and painted. Record early bookings were reported by hotels and guest houses, and Daisy's bistro was full most nights.

She could hardly believe the publicity the village was receiving. The story of the long-lost heir from California was a hot topic and everyone wanted to visit where it was all happening.

Daisy had moved back to her flat a few days after the funeral, but she continued to visit her grandmother most days when she could be spared from the bistro.

One morning Dave Bunt made an early-morning delivery of the fish order.

'I can't keep up with you,' he grumbled. 'You've practically doubled sales since *he* came here.'

'You mean Ben?' Daisy was checking the order. 'We're not complaining. It's all good for business. Hey, there's not enough John Dory here — Martin won't be happy not to have his favourite fish.'

'No, sorry. Christopher took most of the catch for his wholesale trade. Dad sold it afore I could stop him, so I grabbed the best lobsters while his back was turned.'

'That's great. Martin will be placated. We're getting moneyed people down here now and some of them don't bat an eyelid over the price. That's it — all correct. I'll settle up on Friday, but I'll see you tomorrow.'

'Er . . . ' Dave hung back. 'Did you think any more about what I said the other night, before you went up to the Hall?'

'No, no,' she interrupted quickly, 'it's all been a bit hectic. But I just can't take the time off. We're really, really busy.'

'Mmm . . . It's since that new Trevain

came. He's filling Dad's head with ideas about a film to do with the fishing industry down here, so much so that Dad's neglecting his boats and leaving me and Brian to manage them on our own. The whole village has gone crazy since he set foot in Pencreek. I can't think why — some say he's not even a Trevain.'

'Who says?' Daisy spoke sharply.

'Well . . . actually 'twas your dad in the pub the other night. He says he's an impostor. Not that he had many takers for that view, but . . . '

'You shouldn't listen to gossip, and Ben Trevain is going to do a lot of good around here. Dave, I'm sorry but I'm truly busy. Maybe we could talk about this some other time?'

'Maybe. See you then, Daisy.' He scowled as he shut the door with a bang just as Rosie came into the store room.

'What's wrong with Dave?'

'He keeps asking me out, and much as I like him . . . well . . . '

'Poor old Dave. Wow, those lobsters

— does Martin know?'

'I'm just about to tell him.' Daisy thankfully returned to business, always guaranteed to chase tricky personal problems from her mind.

★　★　★

She saw very little of Ben during the next few days; he was occupied with business arising from Harry Trevain's estates as well as familiarising himself with the demands of Harry's various charities. He established his continuing support for Pencreek's male voice choir, and various sports clubs and societies, so that almost to a man the village was very pleased with its new young patron.

One evening just before the bistro closed he came into the bar and asked for Daisy.

'She's in the kitchen helping with the clearing up,' Rosie told him 'We've had a very busy evening, but I'll get her for you. A drink?'

'No, thanks, I just want to talk to Daisy.'

'And here she is.' Rosie smiled.

'Rosie, I think . . . Oh, hi, Ben. It's good to see you.'

'You, too. Sorry I've not been before but there's been a lot to sort out.'

'Yes, I know. I've been busy, too.'

'Have you time now? I know it's late but . . . '

'Sure.' Suddenly the weariness Daisy had been feeling dropped away.

Ben smiled. 'Maybe we could go for stroll if it's not too late. It's a lovely evening . . . '

'OK. I'll get a jacket. Rosie?'

'Nearly done here. I'll lock up — don't forget your keys.'

Rosie watched them leave the bistro — the way Ben held the door open for Daisy, looking down at her as she passed underneath his arm — and frowned. There was something about them — a sort of sparkle? She shook her head, yawned, and closed up the bar.

Outside the air was balmy, the merest breeze rippling the moonlit water. Daisy and Ben walked along towards the outer harbour walls.

'It's a bit different from the other evening,' Daisy said.

'That's for sure. Calm and peaceful tonight.'

They leaned against the rails, looking down into the water.

'Tonight the sea has a smiling face,' Ben murmured.

'It's deceptive. The sea can be cruel, too. In the old days wreckers would lure ships towards the rocks with lights then rob them and even kill the sailors and the passengers. It's not a pretty part of our history.'

'Maybe not, but survival then was so much more difficult. So much poverty . . . '

'Perhaps. You're not doing a film about wreckers, surely?'

He laughed. 'No, that's been done before. I'm interested in the here, the now, and the future — though the past is all part of that.'

'The fishing industry's your subject? That's what I hear.'

'Yes, for a start. I'm meeting Uncle Christopher in a couple of days. We'll be filming at the market.'

' 'We'?'

'The crew arrives in a couple of days, and my PA, Debra, and a cameraman fly in to Newquay tomorrow.'

'Wow! You haven't wasted much time.'

'No. Well, there's a lot to do. Mr Liddicoat's advanced me some finance so we can go ahead immediately.'

For a while they watched the play of moonlight on the water, then he turned to face her. 'Daisy, I've missed you . . . your support . . . '

'We've both been busy.'

'And I'll be even busier when we start filming. I've been up to the Hall each day to see Martha. She's worried about your dad. Have you seen him?'

'Only briefly a couple of days ago. He said he had to meet someone; he didn't stop to talk.'

'Martha says he's been miserable ever since he got back from Spain.'

'Uncle Peter predicted that his . . . um, girlfriend would finish with him.'

'Martha thinks he's ill. She says he's very depressed.'

Daisy sighed. 'I'll go up tomorrow morning. Poor old Dad, he's never been truly happy since my mother died.'

'So your gran tells me.'

'She's your gran, too.' Daisy turned to face him. She looked at his firm mouth, his eyes dark and troubled. 'Ben, what's wrong? There is something, isn't there? Something's worrying you?'

He hesitated.

'Maybe. Look, Daisy, I love it here. Cornwall, Pencreek, the people — it's fantastic. I've so many plans, so much to do before I go back to California, that's if I do go back . . . '

'Not go back!' Her heart was pounding. He couldn't stay here, he couldn't. She caught her breath. 'But your home's there, you have to go back surely . . . ?'

'Do you want me to go away, Daisy?'

'Yes. No . . . I . . . of course not. You're — you're family.'

'Am I? Your father and your Uncle Peter don't accept that I am.'

'They're just furious about . . . '

'About my inheriting Sir Harry's money? It could be more than that. Maybe I'm not Sir Harry's grandson.'

'That's absurd.'

'Is it? I don't look at all like any of you.'

'For goodness sake, you knew Harry Trevain better than any of us, with the exception of Martha. Evidently he spent more time in the States than he did here.'

'Your father and uncle both think I'm an impostor.'

'Forget them, they want the money. I hate to say it about my own flesh and blood but that's the truth of it. They've lived their lives expecting to inherit a fortune. Dad's in debt, so's Uncle Peter, and Christopher, too, from all accounts. But they'll accept the situation in time.'

'I don't know. I wish Martha would open her letter. Maybe there's some clue . . . '

'Oh, Ben, stop it. From what you tell me you and Grandad had a loving relationship and I'm sure he was proud of you. How can you doubt it?'

There was a pause, and he bent to pick up a pebble to throw into the sea.

'You're right. I just got caught up in the rumour machine. I'll be glad when the crew arrives and then there'll be plenty of action. I've been sitting in too many meetings with lawyers and bankers. Thanks, Daisy.' Impulsively he pulled her close and kissed her cheek.

She caught her breath as she felt the closeness of his body before he moved quickly away.

'Sorry,' he said.

'What for?'

'My . . . my paranoia. You've enough to worry about.'

'That's OK. It's what families are for. Any time, Ben.' She was surprised to hear herself speak so calmly. 'It's good to see you, but it's time I was getting back. I've a very early start tomorrow. We're fully booked, but I'll find time to go up to the Hall tomorrow.'

★ ★ ★

'Gran, you've done wonders already.' Daisy watched Martha working among her roses, deadheading, pruning and picking.

'It is much tidier. I've neglected it for so long. But I'm happy out here where I can forget all my problems.'

'Problems? Tell me.'

'Well, there's your Uncle Peter constantly grumbling and mumbling about how unfair it all is, Christopher and Patricia at daggers drawn, and Jack looks terrible, depressed, heading for a breakdown, I fear. Could you speak to him, dear?'

'I will. At least you look much better, Gran.'

'I'm getting along. In a way it's better than when your grandfather . . . It was so odd, him shutting himself away all that time. It wasn't much of a life for either of us that last year He was very troubled.'

'Have you read Grandad's letter yet?' Daisy ventured.

'No. You said to wait.'

'I did, but promise you'll call me if you need to.'

'I promise. You know, it's hard to be sad in this lovely weather; summer's a good time to get back to life. Maybe I'll never read that letter. I rather dread it. Ah, here's Molly with the tea. She's made some scones. Now, Daisy, you're not to worry about me. Just speak to your father.'

Before she left the Hall Daisy went in search of her father but he was nowhere to be seen. Finally she went to Patricia and Christopher's apartment, thinking maybe he'd gone there. She was about to ring the bell when Patricia's angry voice from inside stopped her.

' . . . do something at least . . . use-less . . . Peter and Jack . . . if you don't . . . ' Daisy fled before the door opened and one of them, either Patricia or Christopher, she didn't see who, stormed out.

* * *

Back at the comparative normality of the bistro Daisy found Rosie in a state of excitement.

'Some of the film crew are here! And they've booked in for supper tonight. Martin's creating a new dish — 'Lob-ster Pencreek'. And they've booked one of Dave's dad's boats for tomorrow.'

'My dad hasn't been in, has he?' Daisy was worried. She'd tried his mobile but it was switched off, and he hadn't responded to her texts.

'No, I haven't seen him.'

'I'll try his phone again later. I'd better check this 'Lobster Pencreek' — I don't want Martin to go over the top or neglect his cheaper ends of the menu. How are bookings generally tonight?'

'Full, and a queue standing by their phones!'

'But you managed to squeeze in Ben and his party?'

'Of course. It's good for business. I hope these guys stay on, and there are more crew coming.'

Later that evening the bistro was packed and buzzing. Daisy, as always, was everywhere at once, out front chatting to customers, giving Rosie and Martin a hand, in the storeroom, kitchens and wine cellar. She loved it and her adrenalin flowed.

Back in the kitchen she put on an apron and helped Martin plate up his new creation. Proudly he described Lobster Pencreek: freshly-caught local lobster, plain grilled, served on a bed of aromatic braised fennel with local scallops poached in Cornish wine for a rich cream sauce.

'How's that?' He beamed.

Daisy gulped. 'Sounds rich!'

'Small portions,' Martin countered. 'All ingredients locally sourced — I've put that on all the menus. That's a popular idea these days. Demand's outstripping supply, but I've kept some back for Mr Trevain's party, of course.'

'Of course,' agreed Daisy, 'but don't neglect our regular customers.'

'I shan't.'

'Daisy,' Rosie called through, 'they're here and Ben wants you to meet his . . . er, friends.'

'OK, I'm coming. Good work, Martin, you're a star.'

'I think I'll make Lobster Pencreek my signature dish — perhaps in one of Mr Trevain's documentaries?'

'Oh, please.' Daisy raised her eyes to heaven; this was becoming sillier and sillier, she thought as she went into the dining-room.

'Window table,' whispered Rosie, 'champagne and glamour. They've got menus.'

'Daisy,' Ben called out, standing up, 'come and meet Jake, my cameraman, and Debra, my PA. This is Daisy, she owns the bistro.'

Jake, tall, bespectacled and rangy, nodded. 'You've got a great atmosphere in here. Is the food as good?'

'I think so. I hope you like lobster?'

'Sure do. I was raised in Maine, real lobster country.'

The girl, Debra, was very attractive: well-groomed, dark blonde hair, long, straight and shining, falling over her shoulders, skin-tight black dress, long crystal earrings. She didn't look as if she could tag along with Ben on his jungle expeditions, Daisy thought somewhat uncharitably as she smiled a welcome

'I'm glad to meet you both. I hope you enjoy your meal.'

'Can't you stay and have a glass of wine with us?' Ben asked.

'I'd love to but we're a bit run off our feet tonight.'

'OK, maybe coffee later? Debra and Jake are only here for a day or so, just to get the feel of the place. They'll be back later with the rest of the crew.'

'You're going out with Dave tomorrow — Dave Bunt?'

Ben nodded. 'Yep, early in the morning, then I'm seeing Christopher later at the fish market.'

'Are there lots of Trevains in Pencreek, then? Does the family own the village?' Debra's keen eyes were openly assessing Daisy.

'No, but there are several Trevains in the village. Jago's the local preacher, Jethro's a fisherman — some Trevains are very loosely related. There's quite a number of them in the States, particularly in California.'

'Emigrated when the tin mining industry collapsed,' Ben added.

'But you and Ben are cousins, aren't you?' Debra ignored the social history bit.

169

'Yes, yes, we are,' Ben said.

'Well, that's all right then — it's all in the family.' Debra's smile widened. 'I think Pencreek is real cute, just as I imagined it when Ben phoned me as soon as he arrived here. I couldn't wait to come over.'

'To work, Deb,' Ben reminded her.

'Oh, that, too, of course, but we can have fun as well, can't we? I can't wait to see your little nest above the harbour. The Crow's Nest, it's called, Daisy. I just love it there. Ben, maybe we should invite your cousin round to supper one evening? Maybe some of your other cousins, too?'

Ben frowned. 'I don't think . . . '

'I think your table's ready now,' Daisy said thankfully as she gathered up their menus. 'Enjoy your meal, and I — and our chef, Martin, would appreciate your opinion of our special dish tonight, Lobster Pencreek.'

★　★　★

Daisy's dream, or nightmare, that she had to garnish a conveyor belt of Lobster Pencreek dishes with a piece of live squid, was rudely interrupted by a banging on the back door of the bistro.

'What . . . ?' It was dark outside. She turned on the bedside light and blinked at the alarm clock. Five a.m. Too early. She sank back on the pillows, thinking it was probably part of the nightmare, but then the banging started again.

'Daisy, it's me — Dave. Open up.'

Convinced how that there was a dreadful emergency, she shot out of bed, put on her dressing gown and ran downstairs.

'Dave, what's happened? Is it Gran?'

'No, no problems.'

'Then why — ? It's five o'clock!'

'Sorry. I have to make an early start — but it's your own fault.'

'My fault?'

'That's maybe a bit unfair, but I have to take the new Trevain and his party out in the boats, so I had to do your fish order first.'

'Surely not this early!'

'Tide waits for no man, you know that. Party's to be picked up at the quayside sharp at seven-thirty.'

'Couldn't your dad, or Brian . . . ?'

He shook his head. 'Dad's going to the records office in Camborne to do more fishing research for that Trevain, and Brian's already got a 'round the bay' booking. Anyway, have you thought any more about going out with me?'

'Oh, Dave, don't ask, there's so much I have to . . . '

'Right, I'm beginning to get the message. Pretty hopeless, I'd say. Here's your fish anyway. Lobster goes down well with Martin — and the customers?'

'Absolutely. In fact, you interrupted a nightmare I was having about the things. Leave the order, Dave — I'll put it in the cold room and check it later when I'm wide awake.'

'OK, see you soon then — a bit later tomorrow morning.'

'Yes. Enjoy your trip, though the

weather doesn't look too brilliant — choppy seas.'

'Let's hope they've strong stomachs then.' He looked quite pleased at the thought of a boat full of seasick passengers, particularly including Ben Trevain.

'Oh, Daisy, I nearly forgot — your dad, is he OK?'

'Why?'

'Well, it's none of my business, but he's spending a lot of time at the pub, sometimes with your Uncle Peter but usually on his own. He stays till closing time and the other night when I was hosing out the boat he was weaving around the harbour. I was scared he was going to fall in so I put him in my van and dropped him off at Trevain Hall.'

'Thanks, that was kind of you. I am worried about him and so is Gran. Life hasn't been too kind to him lately, and as I'm sure the whole village knows by now, Sir Harry's sons didn't inherit very much.'

'So I heard.' He shrugged. 'Sir Harry had every right to leave his fortune to who he liked. Bit of a blow, though, to your dad and the rest.'

'It's certainly causing problems, but I expect time will heal.' But Daisy was unconvinced by her own words; the task left to her by her grandad looked more and more like 'mission impossible'.

She put the kettle on, thinking it was no good going back to bed now and that what she needed was a strong cup of coffee to start the day. And the first priority would be to seek out her father.

* * *

As the morning wore on she grew more and more worried about her dad. She'd tried phoning and texting, but there was no response. The bistro would soon be filling up for lunch and Rosie had everything under control.

'Do you mind if I slip out for a while?' she asked Rosie. 'I'm a bit worried about my dad.'

'No problem.' Rosie hesitated. 'Er . . . Piran said your dad was in the pub the other night, him and your Uncle Peter. Your uncle left but your dad stayed until closing time. They practically had to throw him out.'

'Hmm, that confirms Dave's story then. Maybe I should try the pub first. He's not at home, I checked with Gran. Though I'm not sure what to do when and if I do find him.'

'You'll think of something,' Rosie said confidently, 'you usually do.'

Daisy felt far from confident as she walked quickly towards the pub. The trouble was that she knew her father. Since her mother died he'd led such a nomadic life, with his failed marriages and relationships. He was not a happy man, and the huge disappointment of his father's will had obviously been a terrible blow.

Pausing by the harbour steps she saw a familiar boat coming in from sea. It was one of the Bunt boats, one of the smaller ones, bouncing up and down in the swell. She waved and called out as it came into the outer harbour. She could see Ben by the wheel next to Dave. Debra, dressed in rainproof jacket and trousers, long hair streaming in the wind, was also standing by Dave, one hand on his shoulder. As they came into calmer waters of the inner harbour they waved back.

'Hi, Daisy.' Ben moved to the front of the boat. 'What a great morning! Wonderful coastline. We've been right round the point.'

Dave secured the boat and they climbed up the steps.

'Thank you, Dave.' Debra smiled. 'That was wonderful. I sure did appreciate it. Can we do it again soon?'

'I don't see why not.' Dave's eyes were glued to Debra. 'It was my pleasure, and if you'd like to go out again just give me a ring.'

'Great. Give me your mobile number and . . . '

'Debra, this isn't a personal trip,

we've work to do, and so has Dave, I expect,' Ben said.

'Oh, don't be so stuffy. I can have an hour or so — I'll work twice as hard to make up. An evening trip would be good.'

'Fine by me.' Dave gave Daisy a sheepish look, but she was delighted to see him so obviously captivated by Debra. Her only concern was that Debra didn't simply play him along for her own amusement, which seemed a likely scenario.

Ben was frowning. He knew Debra of old. She was an outrageous flirt, and Dave did look very smitten. But then, they were adults, so it was none of his business.

'Can you join us for lunch, Daisy?' he asked.

'Thanks, but I'm looking for my father, and then I've got to go back to the bistro.'

'OK. I'm going to the fish market this afternoon to see Christopher. Debra, I want you to do some research and then . . . '

Daisy left them to it but as she hurried on to the pub she couldn't help noticing that Debra was hanging back to speak to Dave, linking arms with him as the group moved along the harbour towards the village.

Bob, the landlord, greeted her warmly. 'If you're looking for your dad he was in half an hour ago with your Uncle Peter. They had a bit of an argument, Peter left, your dad had another drink, then he left, too. I was a bit worried, to tell you the truth, but he told me he walked from the Hall so he wasn't driving. At least, that's what he said, but it's a fair old step from Trevain Hall to here.'

'You don't know which direction he took?'

'I do, actually. I was going to the cellar to change a barrel and as I was going down the outside steps I saw him leave. He headed for the cliffs, and I had half a mind to follow him because he had that hunched look about him, sort of depressed, but then he suddenly straightened up and set off at a fair pace so I let him go.'

'Which way?'

Bob pointed towards the uphill coastal path. 'Beard's Point. You know, the look-out where . . . ' He stopped suddenly.

'Suicide Leap, you mean? Bob, you don't think . . . ?'

'No. No, no-one's jumped off there for years. You mustn't worry.'

'But he's in a state. I must go and find him.'

'OK, but I'm sure he'll be all right, really. He was pretty animated with his brother. Look, if you're really worried, nip back for your car and take the road to the Point — he can't possibly be there yet. Do you want me to come with you? Mary will hold the fort.'

'No, Dad would hate a fuss, but I'll go right now. Thanks, Bob.'

She went to Piran's garage for her car then drove as fast as she dared towards the road leading to the point. It was a popular picnic spot with open grassland and a winding path down to a sandy cove below. There were already several cars parked nearby, but no sign of Jack Trevain.

She remembered that when her mother was alive they would all come to the cove for picnics. Her dad would fish off the rocks, they would have a picnic, swim and play silly games. She was sure her dad had been happy then, with a loving family life. He and Harriet had planned to have a big family: 'Lots of brothers and sisters for Daisy,' she'd heard him say once, and Harriet, her mother, had laughed and agreed.

For a few seconds Daisy was overwhelmed by childhood memories. Then Harriet Trevain had died very suddenly and very prematurely, and Jack Trevain had lost his world and never found it again . . . and nobody had really helped him. Martha had tried, but Grandad Harry had been absent most of the time. Oh, he'd paid Jack's gambling debts time and time again, but he had put his foot down after Jack's second divorce and issued an ultimatum — he must stop being the travelling playboy, come home, and get a job. He'd been well educated, and although he'd had a terrible tragedy in his life, it was time to learn to live sensibly.

Jack and Harry had had one final, terrible bust-up and Jack had disappeared, coming back only occasionally to see Martha and Daisy, but always making sure first that his father was away from home.

Daisy pushed away the flooding memories as she cautiously peered over the cliff edge. There were only a few people down on the beach, no sign of her dad.

She set off to walk along the cliff back towards Pencreek. If Jack was following the path he should be about five minutes away. Then she spotted him, sitting on the grass at the cliff edge, his legs dangling over the edge.

'Dad — Dad!' She yelled, and began

to run towards him.

He turned, looked startled, then looked back out to sea, and to Daisy it was as if his body was poised to slide over the edge onto the jagged rocks below.

'Dad!' she screamed out. 'Stop! Please . . . wait!'

He seemed to hesitate, gave a brief glance again to the sea, then almost reluctantly stood up and stepped back.

Daisy reached him, pulled him farther away from the edge, then hugged him to her.

'Dad, whatever were you doing? You weren't . . . ' Her voice broke and she began to sob.

Jack put his arms round her. 'Hey, hey, what's up? What are you doing here? Why aren't you at the bistro?'

'Oh, Dad, I was so worried. Bob said you'd been in the pub, drinking a lot. And you do look terrible. I tried to get in touch with you, but you're not answering the phone or my messages. I was so worried about you.' She sniffed and rubbed her eyes.

'Here.' He gave her his handkerchief. 'I'm touched, Daisy, I really am. I thought . . . no one cared . . . '

'Of course I care!' she broke in. 'And so does Gran, but you've been away so long.' Her mobile rang. 'Sorry — it's the bistro. Just a sec . . . '

Jack indicated that they should walk on while she took the call. He still held her arm. She nodded a few times then switched off.

'I have to get back. I'd forgotten — I've got a meeting. I'm really sorry, but it won't take long. It's a couple of guys from London and they've a plane to catch. Why don't you come with me? I can drop you off at the Hall and as soon as they guys have gone I'll come to join you.'

'No. Not just now. I . . . I need some thinking time. I'm not very good company right now.'

'That doesn't matter. You're my dad and I need you.'

'Thanks, Daisy, that's sweet of you,

but you don't need me. You've got the bistro, friends, a life, a future. I have nothing.'

'Oh, Dad, please don't. I can't bear it.'

He patted her arm. 'Don't worry, you go to your meeting. I'm going down to the cove. Remember our picnics there with your mother?'

'I do. I was just thinking about that. Happy days. But you can be happy again, Dad. I'll help, we all will.'

'I think I'm a lost cause. I doubt you can help me. But I promise I won't do anything stupid. I had no intention of jumping off the edge, I'm too much of a coward.'

'Promise me!'

'I promise.'

'And promise you'll talk to me. Tell me how I can help,' she urged.

'We'll see. Off you go to your meeting now. I'll see you later.'

★ ★ ★

Guy met her at the bistro; he was working there during the summer break before he went to America later in the year.

'Did you find him?' he asked anxiously.

'Yes, but he's in a poor state, and I don't know how I can help him.'

'We'll talk later, shall we?'

'It might help. You've a wise old head on those young shoulders, Guy. Hey, would you like to sit in on this meeting? You know practically as much about the bistro as I do.'

'That'd be great. What's it all about?'

Quickly she told him about Sir Harry's last business idea just before he died.

'It was uncanny — he was really troubled and confused, then, clear as day, he mentioned franchising the business. I thought it was mad then, but maybe it's got something. You in?'

'You bet!'

'The men we're seeing run some classy franchises, and not just food.

They help set it up — for a price, of course — but it would be fun, and after your MBA you could be part of the business if you want to stay local, or farther afield if we go ahead with the franchise idea. Let's go and see what they have to say.'

* * *

While Daisy was searching for her father on the cliffs Christopher Trevain was showing Ben around the Trevain fish market, a cavernous building, fairly empty now in the afternoon except for men and women scouring the steel tables and hosing down the floors.

'Early morning's the best time to see it when the fish come in, and the buyers. There's lots of noise then, bargaining, deals being made.'

'What time does it start?'

'About four-thirty, sometimes a bit later. It depends on the tides and the weather.'

'That's an early start for you.'

'Oh, I don't get here that early, I haven't done for years. I have a manager, Graham, though he's not here just now. He's the man to talk to — he knows the workings better than I do.'

'But it's you who owns the business?'

'Huh — once I can clear the debts.'

'Isn't it profitable, then?'

Christopher shrugged. 'It's picking up a bit, but the building needs modernising and expanding. We've got a lot more fishing boats coming in, and the potters — they collect the shellfish: lobster, crab, and dive for the scallops.'

'So there's plenty of fish still in the sea then?'

'There is, but we're bogged down by quotas and regulations. I won't bore you with the details. We're also no match for the huge European processing boats. Graham will fill you in on the details.'

Ben noticed Christopher frequently looking at his watch, and over his shoulder, and was puzzled. The market had obviously done good business that day, and although the actual building needed a lot of work, Ben could see the potential.

'I don't want to take up your time, Christopher, but . . . '

'No, no, that's OK, but I'm not sure how I can help you. What's your film about?'

'It's early days yet, but it's mainly concentrating on the historical and social impact of the fishing industry on this part of the world. You're in the thick of it with a business like Pencreek Fisheries so you could be a valuable source of information.'

Christopher pulled a face. 'I'll tell you something, Ben — I've never been too keen on the business. Sir Harry practically forced me into it when I made a complete mess of my college education. If I could I'd get out, except I don't have anywhere to go.'

'But surely it's interesting, with lots going on? What about your boys, Guy and George?'

'Guy's OK, he'll be fine — he could

possibly take this over, though I wouldn't advise it, not at this moment in time.'

'But I thought you said that profits are going up?'

'Er . . . well . . . ' Again there was the glance at his watch, a nervous air. 'Look, Ben, I'm sorry, something unexpected has come up. I really should have postponed this. Maybe another day? I need to speak to my manager, Graham — he's due back at any moment.'

'Sure. You've given me something to go on, anyway. Perhaps I can take you and Patricia out for dinner one evening?'

'That'd be good. We'll fix it up.' He was edging Ben towards the main door, and Ben could feel the relief as they shook hands before Christopher went back into the market.

Ben made a few notes and was sitting in his car adding a few facts and figures when he became aware of a car pulling up behind him. Two dark-suited men got out and went into Pencreek Fisheries.

It was none of his business, but he recalled Christopher's anxious, shifty nervousness, as though he was expecting something to happen, so on pure instinct he went back into the market, now empty.

Christopher's office was at the far end. He saw the two men talking to Christopher, who was sitting at his desk, paled-faced, fingers clutching the desk edge. Christopher saw Ben, shrugged his shoulders, and beckoned him in.

The two men frowned as Ben opened the door.

'Sorry, sir,' one of them said, 'this is government business — private.'

'I'm Ben Trevain. I think I have a right to know what's happening. Christopher?'

'Of course.' He shrugged. 'Everyone will know soon enough in any case. These mean are from Defra, the government department for rural environment, fisheries . . . '

One of them spoke quickly. 'We are investigating Mr Christopher Trevain on charges of keeping and selling over-quota fish. It's a very serious offence, so, Mr Trevain, if you would come with us . . . '

'You're arresting him?' Ben questioned.

'We're government officials, not policemen. Let's say we want to question him and it would be more appropriate to do it at our offices than here. We're taking away all the books for examination.'

'It's all right, Ben, I've been expecting this.'

'Shall I come with you?'

'No, but you could call my lawyer.' He gave Ben a card. 'And maybe tell Patricia?'

'I'll do that. What is this over-quota fish?'

'It's best we go now, sir,' one of the men said. 'Mr Trevain can contact you later.'

'What happens if it's true?' Ben asked.

'A fine — a pretty hefty one,' Christopher said.

'I'll pay it,' Ben put in swiftly, 'however much it is. It's family money, Christopher — the Trevain inheritance. You're entitled to it.'

'Ah.' One of the men looked at Ben closely. 'So you're the new heir to all this, the fisheries?'

'I'm the heir, but the fisheries belong to Christopher here.'

'You're doing a documentary about the fishing industry? One of my colleagues has been helping you, Jimmy Pengelly.'

'Ah, yes, he's been a great help.'

The man hesitated.

'Look, we'll not be keeping Mr Trevain long, just a few formalities at the office, we've got all the stuff we need. If you'd like to come with us and wait, you can take him back home. We're going to close the fisheries for a day or two, then, depending on what we find out, you can open up again — but we'll be making regular visits. OK?'

'Thank you. I'll follow your car. Christopher, I'll phone Patricia.'

★　★　★

Ben phoned Patricia at home and explained what had happened. 'They're asking him a few questions at the Defra office, then I'm driving him home. His car's at the garage being serviced.'

'Yes, I was going to pick him up. Is he all right? I know he's been very worried lately but he wouldn't tell me anything. Anyway, I'll be waiting. Peter's here, too — he and Christopher were going to play golf.'

'They still can, I don't think he'll be long, and a game of golf may take his mind off things.'

'We'll see. Thank you, Ben, I'm glad you were there.'

Within an hour Ben had collected Christopher from the Defra office in town. He looked more composed and pleased to see Ben.

'You know, I'm glad it's out in the open — I've been worried sick.'

'Do you want to tell me about it?'

'Why not Everyone will know soon enough. I've been a fool. The fishery was operating at a loss before my manager, Graham Browne, took over. I . . . I'm afraid I neglected the business. My heart was never in it and I just let it slide, so when he turned it around, I just sat back, took holidays, played golf, went home early . . . ' He shook his head. 'What a complete idiot.'

'So what have you actually done to have those guys after you?'

'Graham has been selling under-quota fish — 'black fish' it's called in the trade. If a trawlerman or boatman exceeds his quota according to the EU regulations, he must throw back what he's caught over his quota. These are dead fish, useless fish, Ben, no use to anyone.'

'Seems a bit counter-productive.'

'Exactly, but it's the law, and, of

course, fewer fish are caught and sold so the prices are higher. Everyone suffers, but that's the law. The 'black fish' economy is illegal and there are whopping fines if you're caught.'

'So were you . . . ?'

'Not at first. I only noticed that under Graham Browne's management profits were actually going up. Of course, he was taking his cut, but I turned a blind eye — anything to avoid going bust.'

'So this Graham Browne is the guilty party?'

'He was initially, but I'm the boss, the owner. I connived by default, if you like.'

'But they'll be questioning him?'

'Huh! Graham was supposed to meet me this morning. He was supposedly concocting a cast-iron alibi to clear us both, but according to the government guys, when they went to his home he'd gone. It was a rented place, shut up and empty. He has a villa in Spain and a flat in Turkey but I doubt he'll be in either of these places. I reckon he's pulled schemes like this before.'

'They'll surely catch up with him somewhere.'

'Even if they do, ultimately it's my responsibility. I knew in my heart something was wrong, but I buried my head in the sand and tried to forget my troubles on the golf course and with exotic holidays we couldn't afford.' He passed his hands wearily over his eyes. 'Patricia won't be married to a pauper — she'll leave me. As for the boys . . . Harry was right — I'm a failure, and certainly not fit to handle his legacy.'

'Come on, Christopher, we'll work it out together. Charlie Liddicoat will get you a top lawyer and then you can make a fresh start. Pencreek Fisheries has a lot of potential. Get your sons involved. Guy's a business student, isn't he?'

'He *is* still a student though, and the only thing George knows about fish is the price of fish and chips at the local chip shop!'

'We can change all that. George says he'd like to come out to California. I can get him a job at a surf school. And I'll tell you what, I'll put in Trevain money as the price for you co-operating in my filming.'

'Aw, you don't need me, you've got a team.'

'I'll need your local knowledge. You grew up here, you're part of what I desperately want to show on film: the development of a community based originally on fishing.'

'You'd help?' Christopher said in a low voice. 'After what we've said about you? And your aunt? And about us fighting you?'

'Well, that was a natural reaction. You know, maybe it's part of Grandad's plan — maybe he wanted to shake us all up; you know, like a kaleidoscope: shake all the pieces up then watch them fall back into place, better than ever.'

They drew up outside Trevain Hall.

'Thanks, Ben. You'll come in?'

'No, thanks. I've got a lot of stuff to put together at my cottage, and I want to see Guy later at the bistro. Do you want me to say anything to him and Daisy?'

'No. I'll explain. It'll be all over the village soon enough, though all wrong or exaggerated wildly. They've probably already got me locked up as a mass murderer! Lots of people in Pencreek would make great script writers for your films!'

'Oddly enough, I have had a few offers! Fortunately I've got my own adviser and I do most of it myself anyway.' Ben got out of the car and they shook hands. 'Good luck, and try not to worry.'

'Thanks for everything, Ben, and from now on you have my full backing. I accept entirely the terms of Harry's will. I reckon he had all his marbles when he made that — he knew exactly what he was doing.'

★ ★ ★

Peter Trevain, waiting at the Hall and now done out of his game of golf, was far less sympathetic to Christopher's problems.

'You're a fool! You may wriggle out of this one with a caution or a fine if you're lucky, but we're all practically penniless. How are you going to pay for legal representation?'

'Ben's going to pay . . . '

'Pah! That's rich! It's *our* family money. Ben so-called Trevain is generously giving you what's ours. But I'm going to stop him even if I die in the process.'

'Well, count me out,' Christopher said firmly. 'I'm going to ride this out if I can, take Ben's offer, and try again with the fishery and try to be a proper manager.'

Patricia Trevain was silent, but then suddenly she went over to her husband and kissed him.

'I'm with you, Chris, and I'll help you. I've changed my opinion of Ben Trevain, too. I don't believe he *is* an opportunist. He's talked to Guy and George and they're impressed, so I'm sticking with my family. Count me out as well, Peter, with any schemes you have for doing Ben Trevain out of his inheritance.'

Christopher was stunned. 'You mean that? Truly?'

'I do. My boys are the most important thing in the world. To pot with golf, committees, Hunt balls and so on — I'll even work at the fishery if it'll help. I've got a good business head — I've been treasurer to all sorts of village organisations, remember. I can manage the fishery standing on my head. Look what Ben Trevain has achieved since he's been here.'

'You're a pair of fools,' Peter rasped. 'Don't expect any goodwill and philanthropy from me once I've overturned this crazy will, as Jack and I surely will. At least *he's* still on my side.'

As the walls shock with Peter's furious door slam, Christopher put his arms round his wife and kissed her with real love and affection, for the first time since either of them could remember.

★ ★ ★

Back at Pencreek Ben called in at the bistro for a quick word with Guy who was also working with Ben in what little spare time he had. As usual the bistro was busy, practically all tables occupied. Daisy was at the bar chatting to customers when she saw Ben. She caught her breath as he smiled and waved across the crowded room.

'Guy?' he mouthed.

She nodded, pointing to the kitchen, then showed her customers to their table and came back to the bar. Ben was still there.

'Busy night,' he commented.

'Yes. And I hope it will be every night now until the season ends.' She wore a simple black dress, her hair loose around her shoulders, her eyes bright with excitement.

'You love it, don't you?' Ben touched

her shoulder lightly.

'I do,' she said, moving back fractionally.

'I haven't seen you for days and you haven't seen my cottage yet. Can you come over later tonight? A quick drink?'

'Er, I won't finish until late, unless . . . I suppose I could leave early. I'd certainly like to see it . . . but what about Debra?'

'Debra? What's she got to do with it?'

'Isn't she . . . ? I thought . . . ?'

'Heavens, no! Debra and I are workmates, and she's a good friend, but that's all.' He laughed. 'She just can't help herself — she flirts with any man in sight. She's working on your friend Dave Bunt right now.'

'Oh. I hope she doesn't . . . '

'Don't worry — from what I've seen of them Dave is very capable of sorting her out. She's completely fallen for him, and his accent. No, there'll be no-one at the Crow's Nest but me.'

'OK, I'd like to see it, and there's something I want to talk to you about.

I'll try to leave here around nine; the main rush is over by then and Guy will always stay on — he's a good lad.'

'I agree. He's taking to the filming very well, a multi-talented young man.'

'Like his grandad. So, we're not all bad blood, we Trevains?'

'Whoever said you were? Ah, there's Guy. See you later then.'

★　★　★

It was nearly half-past nine when Daisy left the bistro to climb one of Pencreek's winding back streets to Crow's Nest Cottage which was literally perched high above the village like the crow's nest of a masted schooner.

'Sorry I'm a bit late,' she started, then, as Ben opened the front door wider, she let out a gasp. The front door led directly into a small sitting-room. Opposite the door a newly fitted picture window framed a perfect postcard view over the water where yachts, ferry boats and pleasure boats bobbed on a serene grey-blue sea in the soft summer dusk.

'Wow!' she exclaimed. 'What a view!'

'I love this place,' Ben said. 'It's tiny but it's got everything: galley kitchen below, bedroom and study above, even a small balcony outside. It'll be a hard place to leave.'

'You're leaving?'

'Not just yet, but I'll have to go back to the States soon.'

Daisy's heart sank even though she had known it was inevitable.

'I'll be back and forth,' he said, pouring wine. 'Here, to Crow's Nest, and Pencreek.'

They stood at the window. Lights now twinkled on boats and in restaurants below them and neither wanted to break the moment.

It was Daisy who, with a small sigh, turned away to sit on the sofa.

'So, what is it you want to talk to me about?' he asked.

'It's the family — the Trevains. I'm worried about them — us,' she corrected quickly. 'My dad is very withdrawn and depressed, Uncle Peter is still simmering, and Christopher you know about.'

'Sounds like a lot of families I've met.'

'I'm sure we're not unique, but I sort of promised Grandad that I would try to bring harmony and peace. I didn't know what he meant when he asked, but I do now. He asked me to help you, Ben, to be part of the family — I think that's what he meant. Didn't he ever talk to you about us in California?'

'He did, but it was mainly about Cornwall. That's how I came to love it even before I saw it.'

'But you see, don't you, that I have to try to do something?'

He topped up their glasses and sat down beside her.

'We should all get together, that's the first step. A family party, maybe? Some occasion — a birthday?'

'It's Granny's birthday next week, that could be the excuse. We could have a party at Trevain Hall.'

'Wouldn't more neutral ground be better — or outdoors, a barbecue?'

Daisy considered that, and nodded. 'She loves outdoor picnics, and we could have it on Gull Island. She'd love that.'

'Gull Island?'

'It's a tiny uninhabited island a mile or so off the coast from Pencreek. We used to swim and picnic there when we were kids. There's a sort of cave, too, so if it's bad weather we would have somewhere to shelter.

'You're a genius, you know that?' Impulsively she reached to kiss him. Their lips met and the kiss held for seconds before she broke away.

'Sorry,' she said.

'It's . . . OK, Daisy, don't worry.'

'I'd better go . . . '

'No, don't. It's OK,' he repeated. 'We'll have the barbecue, it'll be fun. Can we hire a boat from Dave?'

'I should think so. His dad has bigger ones. We did have a family boat once but that's gone to rack and ruin. A bit like the Trevain family!'

'Come on. You, Guy, George, the young ones, you're all OK, and Christopher and Pat are on track now. Let's give the barbecue a try anyway. Just family, I think, don't you? Except Dave, of course.'

'I agree, just in case there's an almighty bust-up on Gull Island!'

'Don't be such a pessimist, Daisy Trevain.'

★ ★ ★

Martha's birthday was in the first week in July, when the nights were still light until late. Daisy organised the bistro to provide food and drink, and Guy and George would be an advance party during the day to rig up lights and the barbecue. Jem Bunt spruced up his best boat and Dave would be in charge.

Daisy practically railroaded all the Trevains to be there. Only Peter Trevain refused point blank.

'There's no point,' he snapped when

she phoned him. 'Family harmony?' he sneered. 'You're joking! We don't like each other much, and as for spending an evening with 'the impostor' — no, thanks.'

She went ahead in spite of him. Martha was charmed by the idea; it was ages since she'd had an outing, and if Peter didn't want to come, too bad. But Daisy was worried about him; his anger seemed to be all-consuming. He'd abandoned his clubs, both golf and social, and even his search for a rich widow, instead nursing a brooding anger at what he termed 'the great betrayal'.

In early July Daisy scanned the weather forecasts. The month had started hot, dry and sunny, and she agonised over bringing the party forward in case the weather broke, but Martha was set on having it *on* her birthday, so Daisy could only hope the weather would hold.

The day before the party was still fine and warm, but the forecast gave an unsettled outlook with maybe a few squally showers.

'Should we postpone?' she asked Guy anxiously as they prepared the hampers for the following evening.

'Naw, everything's set up and you know the weather here often bucks the trend. We should go ahead. Gran's looking forward to it and in our climate you could dither about for ever. Grasp the nettle, Daisy.'

So she decided to go ahead, a decision she was later to regret . . .

Drama At Sea

A score or so of Trevains assembled at Pencreek's harbour quay on the early evening of Martha Trevain's eighty-third birthday. Since Harry's death Martha had kept in touch with the village Trevains who had been at the funeral. Jethro Trevain, a local fisherman who sold his catch to Trevain Fisheries, and his wife and daughter joined the party, along with Jago Trevain, a local and travelling lay preacher with a reputation for fiery oratory. They'd had little contact with Harry Trevain in his latter years but were pleased to be included now.

Dave had polished up his father's latest addition to his pleasure boat mini fleet. It had a spacious inside cabin, very comfortable seating, and a glassed-in wheelhouse. Dave had also, with Debra's help, garlanded it with

Happy Birthday ribbons. A black and white Cornish flag few aft and the Union Jack at the prow. Before the party set off for Gull Island Martha was piped aboard to the tunes of 'Happy Birthday' and 'For She's A Jolly Good Fellow.' Presents and cards were showered on her in the cabin as soon as the boat cast off.

Daisy hoped for the best after listening to the latest weather forecast: 'possibility of scattered thundery showers towards midnight.' With any luck the party would all be safely tucked up in their beds by that time.'

Preparatory to casting off Dave checked his passenger list, and ticked all but the one who had refused the invitation anyway. But as he signalled release of the moorings there was a shout: 'Hang on, wait for me!' and to Daisy's astonishment Peter Trevain came running to the boat.

'Uncle Peter!' Daisy gave him a helping hand to clamber in. 'Changed your mind? I'm pleased, and your mum will be delighted.'

He scowled. 'I thought I'd take advantage of the free food and drink that he — ' he jerked his head towards Ben ' — is paying for with our money. Jack's here, is he?'

'Of course, and I'm sure we're all set to have a good time.'

Without a word to the others he took a seat on the outside deck beside Jack who was sunk in his usual hangdog gloom. The two lonely men had developed a canker of anger, self pity and negativity.

Young Guy and George, in complete contrast, were smart, bright and athletic looking, the very antithesis of the older pair. George greeted the elder Trevains cheerfully. 'Hi, guys! Glad you made it.'

As they all assembled in the lower deck cabin for a champagne toast to Granny Trevain, Dave's horn blared as he pulled away from the quay and evening strollers cheered and waved them off on what was obviously a special occasion.

As a concession Dave had been allowed to invite Debra as his second mate; she was an experienced sailor whose San Francisco family owned a large motor yacht. As Debra stood with Dave at the wheel Daisy thought they made an attractive couple and felt relief that he had shift his focus from herself to this perky American who had completely captivated him.

The outward journey was pleasant with only a slight swell. The champagne flowed as the Trevains chatted amiably and watched the sun go down as they neared the island, protected by a rocky reef.

Dave had done the trip many times before and had no trouble landing his party via the dinghy on to the wide sandy beach.

Guy and George lit the barbecue, switched on the fairy lights, and started up the music. Guy and Daisy had created a plentiful and imaginative menu, and in between eating, people danced, sang and chatted.

Later George organised a cricket tournament, while the non-cricketers strolled or sat on the sun-warmed stones, dangling their feet in the tepid water of the rock pools.

Ben was one of the hardy souls who opted for an evening dip, swimming strongly away from the rocky reef. Once out of the water, his towel slung round his shoulders, he joined Daisy.

'Well done. It's a great success.'

'Thanks, but it's not all peace and love. I'm worried about Uncle Peter and my dad. Peter looks so angry, and he's had too much to drink — and I think the weather's on the turn.'

'Should I tell Dave and Debra to get ready to go?'

'Probably. They make a good couple, don't they?'

'Mmm. I'm surprised — she's usually flitted on to the next guy by now.'

'I just hope she doesn't break his heart. Dave's such a good guy.'

'You sound kind of wistful. Were you and he . . . ?'

'Oh, no. No, we're good mates from school days, that's all.'

Ben smiled as he looked at her. His strong tanned body held a great attraction for Daisy and she momentarily closed her eyes.

'He's family' — inwardly she repeated the mantra.

'Right,' she said briskly, 'let's gather everyone up and head back to Pencreek.'

'Daisy dear,' Martha came up to them, beaming. 'I've had a really lovely time. Thank you so much.' She had presided over her birthday party like a true matriarch, enjoying every minute of the sort of family occasion she'd missed so much in her husband's reclusive years.

'It so much reminded me of the old days when the boys were young. We used to come to Gull Island often. Good times. I only wish Peter . . . '

'I know, but at least he's here — that's maybe a good sign, though he's not exactly been the life and soul of the party. I've tried to draw him into the centre but he and Dad have obstinately remained on the fringe.'

'You've done your best, dear. Ah, here comes the rain — time to go.'

Along with splats of rain came a flash of lightning and an ominous roll of thunder. The forecast storm was heading their way.

Daisy clapped her hands and called out, 'Come on, everyone, it's time we were off. All hands to clear up. Dave and Debra, will you take Martha, Jethro, Jago and the rest on the first dinghy trip? By the time one of you comes back we'll have everything packed ready to go.'

It seemed no time before everyone was on the boat and ready to head back towards the mainland.

The wind was strengthening as they made for the open sea and waves began to lap and rock the boat. Martha and most of the others retreated to the cabin below while Dave and Debra manoeuvred the craft away from the treacherous rocks. But the boat seemed to make little headway and a strong offshore wind was driving them back towards the island.

Ben joined Dave at the wheel. 'What's happening? We need to get off quickly now.'

'I dunno, we seem to be stuck. I'll take a look. Deb, take the wheel.'

'OK,' but as she spoke there was a bang followed by an ominous crunching and grinding as the boat juddered to a halt.

Several of the others came up from below.

'Why aren't we moving?'

'Is the boat OK?'

Jethro, an experienced boat man, looked over the side.

'There's a lot of weed down there. I guess the prop's fouled. Unless you can shift it from up here someone'll have to go down and free it.'

Dave tried to hold the boat steady as it shuddered and groaned, straining to free itself.

'The storm's worsening,' he commented.

'Maybe we should try to get back to the island, take shelter in the cave,' someone suggested, but at that moment a huge wave caught the boat broadside on. It lurched and slid partially off the encircling reef.

Dave tried the engine again, but they remained stuck. Worse, dark clouds were scudding across the face of a fitful moon, lightning flashed across the sky, and rumbles of thunder crept nearer.

'What next?' yelled Debra, long hair plastered across her cheeks.

'I'll have to go over the side and free the propeller,' Dave answered.

'I'll go,' Ben said. 'You should stay at the helm.'

'Mind the rocks,' Dave cautioned.

'Ben,' Daisy yelled, 'take care.'

He grinned as he gave her a thumbs-up and disappeared over the side.

'Does he know what he's doing?' Peter and Jack came up on deck, staggering against the motion of the boat.

'I hope so.' Dave was peering over the side.

'Has he got a knife?' Debra asked. 'Because if the prop's tangled . . . '

'Yes — watch out!' A huge wave reared up over the side and drenched them all.

'We're helpless in this,' George said. 'I think we should call out the lifeboat.'

'Don't panic,' Christopher said. 'Give Ben time.'

'I'll give him five minutes,' Dave said, 'then I'll send out a distress signal. Unless we can free the prop we're just going to be battered to pieces on the rocks. I'm worried about Lady Trevain.'

'She's OK,' George shouted above a tremendous thunderclap and a blaze of lightning. 'The storm's right above us — a summer squall. But look, the horizon's a bit lighter.'

But the wind was still blowing a gale, the sea tossing the boat about like a cork.

'There's Ben . . . astern.' Dave moved towards him but a squall of rain temporarily blinded him. Then the boat's lights suddenly dimmed to total darkness.

No-one ever knew what happened next. Daisy had a hazy recollection of Ben trying to climb back on board, and dark figures rushing towards him, merging, separating . . . some sort of melee . . . then the lights came up again after Guy had checked the generator — but Ben was nowhere to be seen.

'Ben!' Daisy yelled, running to the spot where she'd last seen him. 'Where is he, Dave? Guy . . . help him, he must still be in the water.'

'Don't panic, Daisy, he must be close somewhere. Get the searchlight from the locker — quick!'

Squally rain blurred their vision. The boat still rocked until Dave restarted the engine which roared into life.

'He's done it, he's cleared the prop. We must move. Everyone to the sides to look for Ben.'

'Where is he?' Daisy shouted, frantic with fear.

Debra came to her side. 'Don't worry, he's a great swimmer.'

'Not in this though,' Daisy pointed out, ducking as another wave drenched them.

'Believe me, he's been in far worse situations, honestly. He's the most resourceful guy I know.'

'There he is!' Peter Trevain pointed. 'That rock, to your right. Pull the boat around.'

'But that's back towards the reef.' Dave frowned, peering through the rain. 'It's nothing,' he said tersely, 'just a heap of seaweed and a plastic bucket.'

'We have to keep looking.' Daisy was frantic. 'He must be here.'

'Daisy, he could be anywhere by now,' Dave pointed out. 'The current's so strong here he could have been swept out to sea. I'm calling out the coastguards. We're just wasting time . . . '

'We can't just leave him . . . ' Daisy was sobbing.

'We can't do any more,' Guy said. 'We'll call out the rescue services.'

Dave nodded. 'I'm heading home. Daisy, check on Lady Trevain — tell her we're afloat, but don't tell her about Ben. Debra, you help me up here. The storm's abating a bit but it's still tricky until we're clear of the reef. The rest of you, keep looking out for Ben.'

Daisy tried to control her fear but her heart was pounding as she went below to Martha. As she went down the steps to the cabin she saw two figures by the stern where Ben had disappeared: her father and Uncle Peter arguing heatedly. With the wind and rain she could only make out odd phrases: ' . . . fool — damned idiot . . . '

' . . . opportunity . . . took it . . . you stood by . . . '

' . . . Dave . . . wrong direction . . . never find . . . '

Daisy's stomach lurched as she clung to the hand rail. Had — no, he couldn't! — had Peter pushed Ben back into the sea after he'd possibly saved all their lives? And her father hadn't stopped him? Had they taken an opportunity to get rid of the heir to the Trevain fortune so they could claim the inheritance? She had to breathe deeply to avoid being sick.

Fighting for control she stepped back on deck and confronted them.

'How could you? How could you do such a thing?'

'What?' Uncle Peter, all innocence, asked, while her father looked wretched, eyes cast down.

'You pushed Ben over the side as he was getting back in, didn't you?'

'Of course not! Don't be a fool, Daisy. Why would I do that?'

'For the Trevain money, that's why.'

'I didn't do it. He fell back. I came here on the trip to make friends. Why else would I have come?'

'To seize any opportunity going,' Daisy snapped.

'You're wrong. He . . . Ben will tell you the truth,' Jack put in.

'*If* they find him. If he's drowned it'll

be your fault, and I shall see to it that you're both held accountable.'

She turned her back on them and went to the cabin below.

★ ★ ★

It was well past midnight when the Trevain party reached the safety of Pencreek harbour. It had been a bumpy ride back but the storm had passed on, leaving a grey drizzle cloaking the village.

The return trip had been subdued. Daisy's main concern had been to keep Ben's disappearance from Martha. She wanted to keep it that way and enlisted Guy's help.

'You keep Granny on board while I get my car to take her back to Trevain Hall.'

Guy put his arm round her. 'You look terrible, Daisy. Gran will suspect something's wrong.'

'I'll do my best to appear normal, but I'm so frightened for Ben. I don't see how he could possibly survive in that sea.'

'Ben Trevain is a survivor — I have a gut feeling he'll be OK.'

'You've got my mobile number?'

'Yes. Will you stay at the Hall tonight?'

'I'm not sure. I'll feel better in the village. It's stupid, I know, but it's nearer if — if anything happens.'

'Daisy, *when* they find him, they'll probably take him to hospital.'

'I can't bear to think of it.' Daisy shuddered.

'Come on, it's not like you to go to pieces. You have to be strong for Granny's sake. We can't have her upset, especially on her birthday.'

'You're right. Oh, Guy, I wish I'd taken notice of that weather forecast. What a fool — it's all my fault.'

He put his hands on her shoulders and gave her a shake. 'Don't blame yourself, that's ridiculous. Go and get your car, I'll stay with Gran.'

'You've got my mobile number?'

'I've told you, yes! Go, Daisy. Get your car. Now!'

She practically ran to the garage to pick up her car and it was only a matter of minutes before she'd manoeuvred it out on to the quay.

'Daisy.' Martha blinked as Daisy came back into the cabin to fetch her. 'Where is everyone?'

'They've gone home, Gran, and that's where I'm taking you.'

'It's been a wonderful birthday, thanks to you — you and Guy and George, you young people. I'm so lucky. Where's Ben?'

'He . . . er, had to dash off. A phone call . . . '

'Really? That's rather late, surely?'

'Well,' George improvised, 'you know film people.'

Martha yawned. 'I must say I'm ready for bed.'

Daisy nodded. 'Come on, Gran, we'll soon have you tucked up.'

Guy and George helped Martha to Daisy's car, while Daisy hung back to say goodbye to Dave and Debra, who instinctively gave her a hug.

'I'm so sorry things have turned out this way, but I'm sure Ben will be OK. I've told you, he's resilient. He's got more lives than a cat!'

'Thanks, Debra, I pray you're right. Is everybody off?'

'Every last one. Your Uncle Peter didn't look too well. And your dad was collared by Jago Trevain, the hell-fire preacher. Perhaps Jago's looking for lost souls!'

'Mmm. Dad's certainly in that category, so good luck to Jago. I must go — but if there's any news, you've got my mobile number?'

'Yes,. I'll let you know as soon as I hear anything. Goodnight, Daisy, and try not to worry. Get some sleep.'

But Daisy knew sleep would be impossible until there was news of Ben.

Martha Trevain chatted to Daisy all the way back to Trevain Hall.

'I really think the outing brought the

Trevains closer together, and that's a wonderful thing, Daisy. In fact, I've invited Jethro and his family up to the Hall for Sunday lunch. You and Ben could join us.'

'I'd love to but Sunday's really busy at the bistro. Maybe after the season's over.'

'Is Ben staying that long? I thought he was going back to the States soon.'

'Mmm. Here we are, safely back home.'

'Lovely. Are you staying the night?'

'I won't, Gran, I must get back. But I'll make some cocoa while you get ready for bed and bring it up to your room.'

As they went into the house Christopher met them.

'Granny, I was worried about you. I had to bring Patricia home, she was sea-sick on the way back. She's never been much of a sailor!'

'I'm sorry. Is she all right now?'

'She's fast asleep — but, Daisy, what's the news?'

'I'm glad she's OK,' Daisy interrupted swiftly, eyes wide, warning him not to say any more. 'We're going to have a drink then I'm off home. Gran, you go to bed, I'll bring your cocoa up.'

'All right, dear. Hasn't it been a lovely evening, Chris? Your two boys were wonderful, too. You're a very lucky man, Christopher Trevain.'

'I am. Maybe the Trevain fortunes are on the turn. Once the fishery . . . '

Daisy coughed another warning; that was another problem she didn't want Martha to worry about, although she was bound to hear about it sometime.

'Ah, yes.' Christopher got the message. 'So I'll say goodnight.' He kissed Martha, then Daisy, but as Martha turned to go upstairs he whispered to Daisy, 'Any news?'

She shook her head. 'I'll let you know as soon as there is.'

'I do hope he's OK. It'd be a terrible thing if . . . '

'Ben's a survivor,' she said, quoting Debra, marvelling at the same time what a change had been wrought in Christopher Trevain. So at least a small measure of family harmony had been achieved. She could only pray that it would not have been at a terrible price.

She took a hot drink up to Martha and sat with her while she drank it.

As sleep began to claim the older woman and Daisy was just tip-toeing out of the room, Martha called her back.

'Daisy, I meant to tell you — I read Harry's letter. Come and see me soon, and I'll tell you all . . . ' and she was asleep.

★ ★ ★

Back at her flat, Daisy found it impossible to sleep. Whenever she closed her eyes she had to snap them open to escape the nightmare visions of Ben, drowned.

As dawned edged away the darkness she rang Dave.

'Daisy? You OK?' he answered sleepily.

'No. Any news?'

'Not yet. We'll just have to sit it out. Try not to worry.'

Daisy felt like she could scream. How could she not worry?

She tried to distract herself by working on the bistro accounts, which did the trick, and she finally fell into fitful sleep with her head resting on her scattered papers.

The musical tones of her mobile jerked her awake. She snatched it up.

'Yes?' Her voice was squeaky with fatigue. '*Ben!*'

'Daisy? Is that you? You sound odd.'

'Ben, where are you? I've been so worried. I thought you were dead! What happened? We searched and searched.'

'I know you did. I was in the water watching you and yelling my head off but no one could hear me for the storm. You were searching in the wrong place, and then I saw the boat move away and I knew I couldn't rely on being rescued by you.'

'But where are you? *How* are you?'

'I'm fine. I'm in hospital but . . . '

'Hospital? Are you hurt?'

'Not at all — just a few bruises and scratches from the rocks. I was just about tipping into hypothermia when the lifeboat found me so they brought me here, but I'm fine. How's Martha?'

'We didn't tell her, and thank goodness there's no need now.'

'Daisy, I want to see you. Can you come and pick me up later?'

'Of course. Are you at the cottage hospital?'

'Yes. They've promised I can go this afternoon.'

'I'll be there.'

Daisy switched off her phone, shut her eyes, and prayed her thanks.

First she phoned Dave, then Guy and Christopher, with the good news.

'I know,' Guy said. 'He just phoned. Isn't it great news? I'm to take him some clothes. But I'll only be away from the bistro for an hour or so.'

'Oh, don't worry about that! I'm going to pick him up later.'

'See you soon then. Rosie says we're fully booked at the bistro tonight — oh, and the franchise guys are back. They're in the area and would like to see you again — and me, actually.'

'Oh. Is that good, do you think?'

'I'm not sure, but it does mean they're taking us seriously. See you later, Daisy. Oh, and I hate to say it, but, 'I told you so'.'

'Right, I should have trusted you. See you soon.'

A shower, hot coffee and breakfast were all Daisy needed to feel completely refreshed, and when Rosie and Martin came in to start work she'd already done a couple of hours' work at the bistro.

'Are the rumours true?' was the first thing Rosie asked. 'I heard the lifeboat had to rescue you all! Stranded on the island, weren't you, with Ben nearly drowned and Dave's boat smashed to bits.'

'You shouldn't listen to village gossip, you know how people exaggerate. We were in no danger. Ben was at one point, but we made it back safely in Dave's boat. It was a bit scary at times, but all's well.'

'But isn't Ben in hospital with a broken leg?'

Daisy laughed. 'Not that he mentioned! I'm picking him up later, so I assume he's got two sound legs to walk on.'

Rosie sighed. 'Well, I'm glad nothing terrible happened. Now, lunchtime today — that walking group are coming in, and I reckon they'll be hungry. They'll have done ten miles on the cliff path.'

'I'll go and check that Martin's got something hearty planned.'

Daisy was delighted to be back at her lovely bistro, thankful that no-one had been hurt the previous night and that Ben was safe! Her heart was singing at the thought of seeing him soon, safe and undamaged.

Before the lunch party arrived she phoned Martha.

'I'm fine, Daisy. I had a wonderful birthday, so thank you again.'

'You're welcome. Gran, did you want to see me about Grandad's letter?'

'When you've time. I know it's a busy period for the bistro.'

'But . . . you're not upset by the letter?'

'Well, it's difficult to say. It's a very loving letter, but it perhaps explains why Harry was so troubled in his later years. I'll tell you about it when I see you, it's difficult over the phone. You haven't seen your father, have you? He didn't come in last night.'

'No. You could phone Uncle Peter — they were together at the end of the evening.' She remembered her harsh words, but they'd deserved it — or had they? She'd assumed Peter had *pushed* Ben off the boat, but maybe *had* fallen himself; the sea had certainly been rough enough.

'Daisy? Are you still there?'

'Sorry, Gran — yes, I'm here. I've got to go now, but I'll phone soon.'

Daisy sighed. It seemed that one problem simply replaced another! But her father had probably gone home with Peter, spent the night there, and both now had monumental hangovers. They had certainly drunk enough!

Her hand hovered over her mobile, then she changed her mind. 'Stop looking for trouble,' she admonished herself,.

* * *

Bistro lunchtime was busy but she managed to get away mid-afternoon to pick up Ben from hospital.

'Hi, Daisy.' He kissed her cheek in greeting. 'Guy brought my clothes but the doctor wouldn't let me out until he'd checked me over.'

'And you're OK?'

'Fine. None the worse for my night on Gull Island.'

'You spent the night on the island?'

'It seemed the only solution, especially after I'd seen the boat disappearing. I swam back to the island and took shelter in the cave.'

'So how did the lifeboat crew find you?'

'I lit a fire, and they saw it.'

'Resourceful! Debra was right — you are a survivor.'

'I like to think so. Is Martha OK?'

'Yes. She really enjoyed her birthday. Oh, and she's read Grandad's letter . . .'

'And?'

'I don't know yet. I'm going to see her later. Ben, what actually happened on the boat when you were almost back on board?'

He frowned. 'I'm not sure. I remember climbing back, and I think it was your father and Peter grabbed me . . . to pull me in, I suppose. Next I knew, I was in the water again.'

By now they had reached the car park. Daisy was about to unlock the door but Ben put out his hand to stop her.

'Just a minute. Look at me, please.'

'What . . . ?'

She looked into his dark eyes. His features were already imprinted on her brain. It was a face she could love, if only . . .

'Do you see a family likeness of any sort?' he asked almost urgently.

'Ben, of course you're a Trevain! You don't have to look like one. What's brought this on?'

'I'm not sure. Maybe it's your uncle's and your father's opposition. Do you see any resemblance?'

'Not really, but then, I don't look like anyone else in the family either.'

'But you do, you have a Cornish look, a family likeness, like your father, your grandmother, your cousins. I'm the cuckoo in the nest.'

'So, if you're not a Trevain, why did Grandad make you his heir?'

He shrugged. 'I don't know. Maybe there's a clue in Martha's letter. Can I come with you to see her? I have to go back to the States soon to put together some of the filming I've done here.'

'But you'll be coming back here?'

'I want to, of course. The place is in my blood, it's part of me — one reason to believe I am a Trevain.'

What Ben didn't say as he looked hard at Daisy was that there was another, secret reason why he needed to be certain of his lineage . . .

Martha's Letter

The story of Lady Trevain's birthday barbecue on Gull Island whirled around Pencreek for at least a week before it was eclipsed by the next interesting rumour. The episode also further enhanced Ben's standing as the local hero, and now he was nick-named Robinson Crusoe of Gull Island!

Because of local interest it was sometimes difficult for his film crew to work in Pencreek. Villagers would offer their services as extras, tea ladies or members of crowd scenes, and in the end Ben decided it was more practical to film away from the village. He had almost finished work on the local fishing industry and was concentrating on the mining section of his series of films.

Because summer was now well under way with a spell of gloriously fine weather, he and his crew set up a camp under canvas near Land's End. The day before he left, he saw Daisy at the bistro. It was lunchtime and for once not very busy.

'Where are all your customers today?' he asked Rosie. 'Have they deserted you?'

'Most of them are at outside tables eating basic stuff: pasties, salads, cold meats. It gives us a bit of a breather in a hot spell. The beaches are packed now but we pick up later in the evening. Is it Daisy you want?'

'Please, if she's not too busy.'

'She's upstairs fitting in some paper-work. Would you like to take her up a cold drink? We've got some home-made lemonade.'

'Mmm, sounds great. I'll have one, too, if that's OK.'

He met Daisy at the top of the stairs.

'Ben! I was just coming down, but come inside. Ah, lemonade — that's just what I was coming down for.'

He set the glasses down on a counter top.

'Nice flat — good view of the car park!'

'We can't all have wonderful views like the one from your cottage. I've never stopped envying you that. I'm quite happy here, though, above the shop. So, what's happening? I haven't seen you around much lately.'

'No, we've been working down at Penzance. We've set up camp there for a few days. It's easier than trying to find accommodation now it's peak season. More fun, too, to be honest. Why don't you come down and visit? Debra was asking after you. Oh, and Dave's coming, too, to find new fishing grounds. At least, that's his story!'

'They're still together then?'

He nodded. 'They look pretty settled to me. I'm still getting over the shock! Daisy, is your father still at Trevain Hall?'

'No. We haven't seen him since Granny's barbecue. It's a bit worrying, but we've had a post card from him from the north, somewhere near Blackpool, so at least we know he's OK. I can't imagine what he's doing there. He hasn't any money, so how he's living I don't . . .'

'He'll come back. He's sure to, it's his home.'

'I don't know why you think that, since he's hardly been in Cornwall at all these last twenty years. Anyway, I can't be worrying about him any more.'

Truth to tell, Daisy did feel uncomfortable about her father, blaming herself for jumping to what may have been an entirely wrong conclusion the night of the storm, and accusing him of it. On the other hand . . . She shook her head.

'So, is this just a social visit? Pleased though I am to see you, Ben, I am a working woman.' She indicated the piles of paperwork.

'Sure.' He finished his lemonade quickly. 'I wondered if Martha . . .'

'Oh, of course — the letter! Martha

hasn't mentioned it, and I forgot. It's awful of me but I've . . . '

'I know — you've been busy. How are things with the franchise men?'

'That's interesting, too, but I'm not sure. Franchise restaurants are big in America, aren't they?'

'Sure. Places like Red Lobster, Sizzler, Dunkin' Donuts . . . They're nothing like your bistro, but they work. People know what to expect and they get it. But your bistro is unique — I can't see it as a franchise.'

'Guy and I are just looking at the idea.'

'He's interested?'

'Guy's interested in most things — razor sharp, good personality . . . '

'He'll do well in the States. His college is quite near to us in San Diego. And George will be coming out, too.'

'Oh.' Daisy was horrified by the pangs of jealousy she felt, as sharp as a physical pain. A whole year near Ben!

'Are you all right?' Ben asked. 'You look like you're in pain.'

'Oh . . . it's just . . . er, a sensitive tooth. The lemonade. Anyway, I should be going downstairs to help with the lunches.'

'And Martha?'

'I'll phone right now if you can wait, and that guarantees I won't forget. How about later this afternoon if she's free?'

She dialled Martha's number. 'Hi, Gran — it's Daisy. Yes, I'm fine, thanks. Gran, remember you mentioned you'd read your letter? Do you still want to talk to me about it? You don't have to, I know it's very private . . . ' She listened for a while, nodding her head.

'Yes, I'd love to look at the roses, too. Tea-time? Yes . . . um, Gran, I have Ben here and he's a bit concerned . . . ' She stopped and looked at Ben, who held out his hand for the phone.

'Hello, Martha. I know it's a bit of a cheek but I'm . . . Yes, sure, I'd like to see the roses, too. A cream tea? With Molly's scones? Wonderful.' He passed the phone back to Daisy with a puzzled frown.

'OK, Gran, see you later, then. Yes, we'll both be there.'

Daisy couldn't help a giggle as she ended the call.

'She'll be delighted to see us both. The letter? Oh, that! It was as though she'd forgotten all about it. She's more interested in her rose garden than she is in Grandad's letter.'

'Well, that shows she's moving on, surely?'

'I hope so. You know, maybe we're all setting too much store by this letter, looking for answers we won't find.'

'It'll be a start, though. Thanks.' Impulsively he gave her a hug, and both jumped back as though scorched. They looked at each other, startled, confused.

Ben swallowed. 'Shall I pick you up this afternoon?'

'I suppose so. Thanks,' she added politely, trying to erase that burning moment when the dangerous spark of fire had ignited.

★ ★ ★

Sitting in Martha's now restored rose garden which was in brilliant bloom, Daisy began to believe that she had imagined that spark between herself and Ben. They had both been scrupulously careful not to touch in the car, and had kept their conversation politely banal.

It was a relief when Martha met them on the front drive. She embraced them warmly, linked an arm with each, and led them round the house to the gardens at the back.

'Goodness,' Daisy exclaimed, 'what a transformation!'

Martha looked pleased. 'We've engaged a team of young professional gardeners. Gardener's Delight, they call themselves. Haven't they done well?'

'It's unbelievable! I thought the drive looked a bit different, too.'

'Oh, they've hardly started on that, they've been concentrating their efforts here. Aren't the roses just fabulous?'

'Beautiful, but the whole thing is — the lawns, the borders, and is that a

247

water garden before the meadow?'

'In embryo, yes. I'll show you round after tea. Patricia wanted to join us but she had to go to the fisheries to do some paperwork.'

'She really is going to work there? With Christopher?'

'Yes, if all goes well. They've found that Graham fellow in Morocco and he's being brought back. I hope we may get away with a fine if we're lucky. Pat seems to love working at the fishery, and she's helped me with the garden, too. And,' her face lit up, her eyes sparkled, 'you know what we're going to do? We're going to open the garden to the public next year. Just for a few days a week to start with. James, the head of the gardening team, says they're going to work on the camellias, make them a special feature — maybe even get on the show circuit . . . Ah, here's Molly with her home-baked scones for the cream tea.'

'You've lots of plans then?' Daisy was delighted by Martha's positive attitude.

She was a different woman from the careworn person she had been during Harry Trevain's retirement from the world.

'I'm glad, really pleased,' Daisy enthused, 'and I think opening up the gardens is an excellent idea.'

'Ah,' Ben put his cup down, 'so we'll have another string to the Cornish documentary bow. Hidden gardens, eh? There must be a lot more gardens like this hiding their beauty from the world, but that people would love to see, especially if they come with cream teas as good as this one.'

'I'm sure there are, Ben. Do you know, that's a splendid idea — hidden gardens with cream teas. I could look them up on the internet and compile a sort of list of West Country hidden gardens.'

'It's been done, I think,' Daisy said, 'but anyway, you don't have a computer.'

'Oh yes I do! George and Guy have bought one for me and given me lessons. It's great fun.'

'A computer?' Daisy could hardly believe her ears. Of course, Harry Trevain had worked with computers for years, but there had never been one at Trevain Hall. She marvelled at the change in Martha.

It was only after her grandmother had revealed a whole raft of things to do in the future and they'd eaten several slices of Molly's cake on top of the cream tea that Daisy broached the subject of Harry's letter. Martha herself seemed to have forgotten that that was the main reason for their visit.

Daisy shook her head as Martha raised the teapot. 'No, no more tea, thanks. I need to get back to the bistro soon, but do you want to talk about Grandad's letter, or is it too painful?'

'The letter? Oh, I quite forgot! I'm sorry, dear, here I am burbling on about my plans. I'm longing to hear how Ben's filming is going, and the bistro, too, of course. Are you . . . ?'

'The letter, Gran.' Daisy was firm.

'Unless it's too painful?'

Martha poured herself more tea. 'It's difficult. No, not because it's painful, it's just the opposite. A release, in fact.'

'A release?'

'Yes.' Martha took a sip of tea. 'Ugh, cold.' She tipped it on to the grass.

'I thought it might be,' Daisy said wryly. 'Shall I get you some more?'

'No, let me tell you about the letter.'

'You're sure you don't mind my being here?' Ben asked.

'Not at all, though I don't know if you'll hear anything you don't already know.'

'It may help fill a few gaps,' Ben said.

'I doubt that. You see, it's a very personal love letter — a love letter that has finally released me from the burden of fear and ignorance.'

'How . . . ?' Daisy started to say but Martha held up her hand.

'Let me tell you Harry's story. It all started when Harry was posted to America towards the end of World War Two. He was just twenty-four, and we had been happily married for four years. We were in love, I never doubted that. I desperately wanted children, but Harry said we should wait until the war was over. He had a premonition, quite wrongly, that he wouldn't survive.

'What you must never forget is that your grandfather was a good Christian, a God-fearing man who had a quite rigid belief in what was right and wrong. His terrible problem was ... well, he fell in love in America, desperately and passionately, with a young girl called Ava. Your grandmother, Ben.'

'Ava Trevain.' He leaned forward. 'She died. Aunt Helen's older sister. I never knew her.'

'She was much older than Helen, apparently. Don't forget, my dears, I never knew any of this until I read Harry's letter.'

'Oh, Gran!'

'It's all right, Daisy. The letter explains a lot: why Harry spent so much time in America, why he was so conscience stricken. He tried to end the affair but they had a child to consider, Percy.'

'My father.' Ben frowned. 'I was a baby when he and my mother died in Africa. They were missionaries. Aunt Helen adopted me.'

'Harry's letter only deals with his love for Ava and his agony at loving two women, neither of whom he could abandon. Even when Ava died, there was the child, and then you, Ben.'

'So Grandad was leading a double life all this time?' Daisy said.

'He was. He tried several times to make a choice and he came home for good after the war. I was pregnant with Peter by then. But you see, Harry had developed so many business interests which took him to the States, especially California. In his letter he poignantly describes his turmoil, his despair. When he was here with me all he thought about was Ava and Percy, and when he was with her in America it was me and our sons that were nagging at his conscience.

'In the end the strain killed him, first mentally, then physically. It was fine when he was absorbed in his business projects, he could forget us all then, but as he grew older and business became too much for him, his big disappointment was that his sons showed no inclination to follow in his footsteps. Harry was finally a man destroyed by his own conscience.'

'That's awful!' Daisy shook her head. 'A terrible story. And that's all in the letter?'

'Well, no, the letter is quite brief. Just the bare facts about a second love and their home in the States — and don't forget how much he loved America and its whole way of life. It all added to his torment.'

'But I don't understand,' Ben said. 'All this, yet you're so happy?'

Martha laughed. 'Strange, isn't it, but you see, I always knew there was something wrong. I suspected there was someone else — the secret of my husband's soul. If he'd told me I could perhaps have helped him. I don't know. I only know he always loved me just as I always loved him. And I know it's entirely possible to love two people at once, though obviously to a man like Harry it was purgatory.'

'Well, I can't take it in,' Daisy said.

'Perhaps I shouldn't have told you, but because Ben turned up, and his Aunt Helen, you know half of the story, and I'm sure Harry would be at ease if he knew it was out in the open.'

'I don't think anyone else apart from the family should know just yet, though,' Daisy said firmly. 'You know what the village is like.'

'I agree. It's purely a Trevain affair. In fact, I don't think it would help anyone else in the family to know it at all. Jack and Peter have their own problems, as has Christopher. Let's leave it for a while between the three of us. But I had to tell you, Daisy, and you, Ben, as you are Harry's heir.'

'So I am, without any doubt, Harry

Trevain's grandson?' Ben said. 'That's what he says?'

'Not in so many words, but if Ava was your granny and Percy her son, and you are Percy's son, then yes, you are Harry's grandson and heir to the Trevain wealth. Is it too much of a burden, Ben? You don't look overjoyed.'

'It's . . . strange. Growing up, Aunt Helen and Uncle Barrie were parents to me. I only rarely saw my real parents on their home visits. Their lives were dedicated to missionary work. They just flitted in and out of my life, as did Grandad — but he always talked a lot about Cornwall.

'I just accepted it, a man with two families, and when Aunt Helen told me he was dead and that I must go to the funeral, that was what I did. Sir Harry was more like a favourite uncle. I knew he was my grandfather, but I always called him Harry.'

He turned to Daisy. 'That's why I suppose I don't really feel like a Trevain, although I have the name.

Aunt Helen and Uncle Barrie adopted me officially, yet they never changed my name.'

Daisy went to kiss Martha's cheek. 'Thanks, Granny, for telling us. I can see the letter has made you happy, so that's good.'

'It has. It was a letter full of love for me, and sorrow for his last years, too.' She shook her head. 'Such a waste. If only he'd told me before. But you see, now I can be happy and enjoy every minute of what time I have left. It's like a new lease of life, though probably a short one.'

'Don't say that! You've got years left to enjoy. You've got lots of plans, and don't forget our trip to the States next month.'

'I've told Aunt Helen you're going to California and she's going to write to you,' Ben put in.

Martha smiled. 'I'll look forward to that.'

'What did you do with the letter?' Daisy asked.

'Er . . . I burned it. I didn't want anyone, ever, not even you, reading it. It was very personal and private . . . '

'Of course. That's exactly what I would have done,' Daisy assured her. She looked at her watch. 'It's time I was getting back . . . '

Both Ben and Daisy were quiet on the drive back to Pencreek, each coming to terms with the new information about their grandparents.

On the outskirts of the village she said, 'I can't quite believe all that — Grandad and a double life. It's like a movie, or a novel.'

'And we're both involved. We lived on opposite sides of the world, each believing Harry Trevain was our grandfather.'

'Well, he is. It's all that other baggage — Ava, your grandmother . . . Do you think he married her?'

'If he did it was never mentioned. I never saw any photographs or certificates or anything.'

'Not of your grandmother — Ava?'

'Well, yes, when she was very young and very pretty.'

'And your parents?'

'No. To tell you the truth, as a little boy I was scared of them! They were frighteningly grim people. I always felt they disliked me. It sounds awful but I was actually relieved when they died. Aunt Helen and Uncle Barrie have been great parents. You'll meet them both when you visit California.'

Daisy smiled sadly, then shook her head. 'But I'm no nearer achieving Grandad's dying wish for family harmony, am I?'

'You're not doing too badly. Christopher and Patricia and their two lads seem to be getting their act together, and Martha's a changed woman. What more do you want?'

When they reached Pencreek there was a long queue of traffic on the main road.

'It'll be the usual summer snarl-up in the centre, I expect. Drop me here, Ben and I'll walk in.'

'OK. Thanks for taking me to see Martha.'

'I'm glad you were there, and . . . ' Hand on the door she turned back to him. 'We can be good friends, can't we?'

'I don't believe we have any other option, Daisy,' he said sadly.

Fond Farewells

August — peak season for the tourist industry, and Pencreek was no exception. Accommodation was fully booked, the streets and beaches packed in constant summer sunshine. Very often in the last weeks in August the strain began to tell; long hours of work in the restaurants and bars took their toll generally, but not in Pencreek. The village had had a splendid and profitable season, enhanced by Ben's filming crew and the publicity surrounding the 'surprise American heir to the Cornish Trevain fortune.'

Another Trevain spin-off was Martha's garden, which was already open to the public for one day in the week and on Sunday afternoons. Guy had had the idea of attracting visitors to the garden as a blueprint for the future. Working with the Gardener's Delight team, he had set up a competition for ideas for the development of the garden. Maps and sketches could be submitted by members of the public, and each year a prize would be given for the most imaginative idea, which would be implemented by the gardening team.

'The gardens are pretty now, a lovely spot to wander and picnic in. In a few years it will be stunning, and visitors will come back every year to check on progress. Gardening is in,' business-aware Guy told Martha, and she was delighted to agree.

The bistro had flourished. Daisy had had to shelve the franchise idea for a while to concentrate on getting through the busy season, but Guy had had another bright idea — a mini bistro-cum-tearoom at Trevain Hall, supplied from the main bistro. Already he had had plans drawn up for the disused stable block, and even George was showing some enthusiasm in the local Trevain enterprises.

Yet Daisy herself felt strangely out of

sorts, a little left out of all the new plans. She blamed the relentless August grind, which she had always enjoyed before. Somehow the joy seemed to have gone. She felt restless and tired, and even uncharacteristically snapped at Rosie for no good reason, though she swiftly apologised. 'I'm sorry, I don't know what's the matter with me.'

'You need a holiday. At least you're off to the States soon with Lady Trevain.'

'In a couple of weeks. But maybe it's a bad idea. Will you manage?'

'I thought your grandad had taught you that no-one's indispensable; a good ship will run under its own steam. You've not had a proper holiday since we opened two, no, three seasons ago. It'd be an insult to your staff if you didn't push off. Don't you trust us?'

'Oh, Rosie, of course I do! And I'm going to give Granny a break, too. She's never been out of Cornwall, would you believe? Mind you, whether I'll be able to prise her away from her beloved garden . . . '

'It's going well?'

'It's amazing! She looks ten years younger, has bags of energy, and is providing full-time jobs for all Molly and Sam's family. The place is buzzing. It's wonderful.' And, she thought, her grandfather would have thoroughly approved of all the business generated by today's young Trevains.

Ben was well satisfied with his filming. Daisy had seen little of him in the last few weeks. He'd phoned a couple of times from Penzance, the last time to say he was coming back to his cottage for a final week or so before going home to California.

As she and Rosie were putting the final touches to the lunch tables, Daisy's mobile rang. It was Ben.

'Daisy, I know you're busy so I won't keep you, but can you spare an hour to meet me at the cottage tonight, if you're not too late finishing at the bistro?'

'Sure. I can leave early. Rosie keeps

trying to send me off — practise for when I'm in the States, she says. I think she and Guy are planning a secret take-over bid when I'm miles away! Are you OK? You sound a bit down.'

'It's Aunt Helen. She keeps e-mailing me to come home and that's not like her. I think there's something on her mind.'

'Your Uncle Barrie perhaps — could he be unwell?'

'He did have a minor heart attack a couple of years back but he's fine now as far as I know. Oh, and Aunt Helen wants to know the dates when you'll be in California. She wants you to stay with them.'

'Lovely. I'll e-mail her. We'll talk tonight, Ben.'

'OK. See you at the cottage. Er . . . Daisy? I've missed you.'

'Me too, Ben.'

Daisy put the phone down. It would be good to see Ben. She suddenly felt much more cheerful as she went back into the bistro.

'Rosie,' she called out, 'let's have a party before we go off to America, a send-off for the film crew — they've been so good for business. We'll have it here, close up for an evening!'

'Was that Ben you were talking to?'

'Yes, why?'

'Oh, nothing. That's a brilliant idea — a party's just what we need. Hey, do you know what I've heard on the grapevine? That Debra Boone's parents are coming to Pencreek. And you'll never guess why.'

'Not to meet Dave's family? Wow! Are they . . . ?'

'Nobody's saying, but have you even caught a glimpse of Dave around here lately?'

'Hey, you're right. How perfectly splendid!'

'You don't mind? I did think at one time that he was more than a little fond of you.'

'Perhaps, but I'm really pleased for him. It would be wonderful, truly, though we'd all miss him being around.

I can't imagine him living on the other side of the world.'

'We're perhaps jumping the gun?'

'OK, no more speculation. Let's sort out the party and whatever you do, don't forget to invite the Boone family!'

★ ★ ★

Later that evening Ben and Daisy sat outside the Crow's Nest on its tiny patio overlooking the harbour. Ben poured cold white wine and produced a tray of savoury snacks.

'How elegant!' Daisy exclaimed. 'Where did you get these?'

'From a deli we've been using during filming. Good, aren't they?'

'Brilliant. We should send Martin down there to get some ideas.'

For a time they sat in companionable silence, enjoying the warm night air and watching the boat lights twinkling in the harbour.

'I shall miss, this — Pencreek, the

Crow's Nest . . . ' Ben mused.

'You're not going for good, though, are you?'

'No, no, of course not, but it's been such a good summer and I really do feel I'm part of the community.'

'You're certainly that. But something's bothering you, isn't it? Why did you ask me round tonight?'

'Nothing's bothering me. It's just that I have to go to California for a while, and I'll miss you. I . . . I just wanted to see you.'

'But we'll meet up in San Diego at your aunt's, and we're going to have a party at the bistro before you go.'

'What a good idea. When?'

'Next week. Monday. We're closing at nine o'clock. Will all the film crew be able to make it?'

'I shouldn't think anything would stop them. We all fly back on Wednesday, so that's fine.' He topped up their wine. 'Daisy, there is one hing I wanted to talk about — I'm thinking of buying the cottage. The andlord wants to sell. Do you think it's a good idea?'

'Brilliant. It means we'll see you here often.'

Part of her was thrilled, but she also felt apprehension. It would be impossible to forget him if he had a *pied a terre* here. And yet she had to push away these impossible feelings and concentrate on nurturing a friendship between them based on their family relationship. She must settle for that.

He took her hand. 'We'll always be friends, won't we?' he said softly, echoing her thoughts.

'Of course,' but sitting so close to him in the soft darkness she wondered whether it could possibly work. Her feelings were growing in intensity for Ben Trevain. It was an impossible situation.

But for the moment she let her hand stay in his. She would worry about it after the holiday.

★ ★ ★

At the bistro the farewell party was in full swing. There was a happy sense of work well done and the film crew were looking forward to rejoining their families in the States. Martin had excelled himself with a cold buffet of locally-sourced savouries. The music was loud, and a floor area had been cleared for dancing. Martha Trevain had put in a brief appearance at the beginning of the party, but had left early to finish her packing. She and Daisy were leaving for Heathrow in the morning.

Daisy and Rosie were kept busy at the bar and buffet and Daisy didn't notice the figure that slipped unobtrusively into the party. For a moment he stood looking round in bewilderment as though he'd stepped into the wrong doorway. Then Daisy noticed him.

'Dad!' She rushed to hug him. 'Thank goodness! Where've you been?'

'Pretty well all over the country, love. I'm sorry I haven't been in touch properly.'

'What have you been doing?'

He put his hand to his ear. 'It's a bit noisy in here. I didn't know you were having a party.'

'We're off to the States in the morning, Granny and me. Have you been up to the Hall? She'll be so pleased to see you. I could drive you. Do you want a drink first?'

'No, no. I've . . . well, I've given that up, and cousin Jago's outside. He'll take me up to the Hall.'

'Cousin Jago?'

Jack nodded. 'I've been travelling with him on one of his preaching tours — helping the homeless, that kind of thing. Talking to him has made me realise how self-absorbed I had become. I'm going to apply to go to college — train in social work, to try to help others.'

'Oh, Dad!' She threw her arms around him. 'That's just wonderful. You're serious?'

'Never more so. I've wasted the best part of my life so far. I'm going to ask your grandmother for a loan to clear my debts and pay for college, but I'll pay her back. Daisy, I don't think I can stand this noise — I'll see you at the Hall tomorrow, before you go.'

'Sure. Dad, I'm so pleased.'

He nodded. 'Me too. Oh, and give my best wishes to Ben, he looks too busy to speak to me right now. Tell him . . . tell him I'm sorry.'

'Well!' Daisy rejoined Rosie at the bar. 'What a surprise!'

'Tell me later — I've a feeling we're about to have another surprise.'

Dave Bunt had clapped his hands for silence.

Debra Boone, in a scarlet figure-hugging linen dress, long hair like sheer silk tossed over her shoulders, was standing next to him. Their hands were clasped together, Dave's other arm fondly round her tanned shoulders. Mr and Mrs Boone looked proudly on.

'Sorry to interrupt the fun, everyone, but I can't keep this to myself any longer. I've asked Debra's folks here if I may ask their daughter to marry me. Thankfully they've said OK, so I'm asking Deb right now in front of all my friends and family.'

He turned to Debra, put both hands on her shoulders and said softly, 'Debra Boone, you will marry me, won't you?'

For a second Debra closed her eyes. It was so quiet you could hear a pin drop. Then, with a wide smile, she put her arms round Dave's neck.

'I sure will, Davey Bunt, and no-one's going to stop me.'

They kissed to tumultuous applause. The music started up again to the strains of 'Here Comes The Bride' and the party went wild. Daisy ran over to the smiling pair to join in the congratulations.

Dave looked embarrassed. 'I . . . er, Daisy . . . '

She kissed him and hugged Debra. 'I'm so pleased for you both, but surely you won't bc leaving us?'

''Fraid so,' Charlie Boone joined in. 'Sorry, folks, but Davey will be joining my deep sea fishing outfit in Florida. Mamie and I just love him to bits and he'll be a wow with the tourists.' He clapped Dave on the shoulder. 'I'll go get us a bottle of bubbly. You'll join us, Daisy?'

'Of course. I wish Dave wasn't leaving us but . . . that's life.'

'We'll be back. Deb loves it here, but think of it — deep sea fishing in Florida! That'll be a real adventure.'

Ben joined them, congratulated the happy couple, then kissed Daisy on the cheek.

'Thanks for a great party. See you in San Diego.'

Daisy nodded. She had mixed feelings about San Diego, but she knew she had to go.

$$\star \quad \star \quad \star$$

It was well after midnight when the last stragglers reluctantly left the bistro but finally only Rosie and her husband, Piran, the Boones and Dave were left.

The senior Boones, Charlie and Mamie, couldn't hear enough about Pencreek, the Trevains and in particular Trevain Hall.

'We plan to stay a while,' Mamie said. 'We might even buy one of those dear little cottages we saw coming in, perched on the hill above the harbour. Then, once Debs and Dave are married, they'll have a holiday home for when they visit Dave's folks.'

'We're only just off the plane at Newquay,' Charlie said. 'We came straight here, so we haven't met Dave's folks yet. That's for tomorrow, eh, Dave?'

'I hope so. Mum's been cooking lunch since yesterday!'

'It's time you got back to your hotel, Mom and Pop,' Debra said firmly. 'You must be real beat — jet lag tomorrow.'

'I don't suffer from that. I don't believe in it,' Charlie said cheerfully, 'nor does Mamie. Now, Daisy, we're in England for three weeks — will you be back home before we leave here? We'd sure like to visit Trevain Hall.'

'I think so. Is Debra staying on, too?'

'No, she's due back in the States to work. She's here for a couple of days more though. After that, Davey's going to look after us, aren't you?'

'I'll do my best. Dad will show you around, too.'

'Perfect. Well, we'll wish you all goodnight, and, Miss Daisy, you have a great time in our country. Have you been before?'

'Yes, I spent some time after college working in the restaurants, building up my practical skills.'

'Well, have a happy visit, and you can be sure we'll be patronising your cute bistro during our stay.'

Dave and Debra were allowed a goodnight kiss before the ebullient Boones swept their lovely daughter off to stay a couple of days with them at their hotel.

'Well,' Rosie sat down, 'what a turn-up, Dave! Or should we say Davey now? You sly dog! Florida marries

Cornwall, eh — what will your parents think of that?'

'They love Debra and they're already planning a trip to Disneyland. Anyway, what's wrong with Florida hooking up with Cornwall?'

'Nothing, Dave.' Daisy patted his shoulder. 'We think it's great.'

'Er, Daisy . . . ' He looked embarrassed. 'I know I asked you out and, honestly, I was serious, but then I met Debra and . . . well, that was it, it knocked me sideways! Nothing like it's ever happened to me before.'

'There's no need to explain.' Daisy laughed. 'I know Debra felt just the same. We're only sad because we may lose you and Pencreek'll never be the same, will it, Rosie?'

As they spoke they cleared glasses and plates through to the kitchens where Piran was operating the dishwashers.

'Time for bed.' Daisy yawned. 'I've to be up at the crack of dawn and I haven't finished packing yet.'

'Goodnight, Daisy.' Dave gave her a hug. 'Thanks,' he said, 'and have a great trip.'

'I will — and congratulations. You and Debra, it's great.'

'Who'd have dreamt it?' Rosie said when he'd gone. 'It's certainly an unlikely combination.'

'It'll work, though. They're totally in love.'

'I think it's sweet. What time are you leaving tomorrow?'

'Late morning. I'll be here for a bit, then I'll pick up Martha, drive to Heathrow, stay overnight and we're on the early morning flight to Phoenix.'

'Phoenix? That's Arizona. I thought you were going to California?'

'We are — via Nevada for the Grand Canyon and Las Vegas, two places Gran specially wants to sea. San Diego's our last stop for a bit of sight-seeing, then we'll be staying with the Thompsons, Ben's aunt and uncle.'

'Is that Ben's home?'

'He has his own condo nearby, but

they're both in a place called La Jolla, a really posh suburb of San Diego, apparently.'

'Sounds fabulous! I bet you'll have a great time.'

'I'm sure we will. And thanks for everything, Rosie — tonight . . . '

' . . . was fun. Make sure you keep in touch: postcard, e-mail, the usual stuff.' Though tired, Rosie seemed reluctant to leave. 'Daisy . . . will you be seeing Ben?'

'Probably, since we're staying with his folks. Why?'

'Oh, it's just . . . OK, Piran, I'm coming. I've got to go, Daisy. You take care now.' She hugged her friend fiercely. 'And don't forget those post-cards!'

Now Daisy was alone. After the party everything seemed eerily quiet.

It felt odd — no more bistro for over two weeks, when it had completely occupied her life for the last three years, a dream made reality thanks to her grandfather. It was certainly time she took a break and it would be fun to show Martha a different country, a country where Harry Trevain had had his strange double life. Perhaps Martha would find it painful, but she had quickly become reconciled to life without Harry. Daisy hoped for the best.

She went up to her flat, made coffee, and did a speedy packing job before having a shower and going to bed. Her last waking thought was guilt-tinged. She'd quite forgotten about her father's visit to the bistro and what he had told her. She would think about it tomorrow.

★ ★ ★

When Daisy arrived at Trevain Hall next morning Martha was packed and ready to go, her bags at the door.

'Hello, Daisy, I'm so excited! You can put your car in the garage — your father's going to drive us to the airport.'

'Hi, Daisy.' Jack Trevain started to load the bags into the boot of Martha's car. 'Change of plan. I'll meet you when you come back, too. It'll be less stress and strain on you both.'

'But, Dad, I don't mind . . . '

'Please, Daisy, I want to be more useful, more of a son . . . and father. Let me try — please?'

'Well, sure, that'd be great. I'll be delighted not to have to drive all that way. Thanks, Dad!'

'I'm giving your father my car anyway,' Martha said. 'I hardly use it nowadays.'

Daisy was pleased to see her father sober, serious and with a determined purpose. She just hoped it wasn't a flash in the pan, and that he really had found a way forward in his life.

While Jack and Daisy stowed the luggage, Martha looked wistfully at her lovely rose garden.

'Gardener's Delight say we could open up two or three days a week in

September now. I can't wait, it'll be so exciting.'

'I hope your trip will be exciting enough to make you forget Trevain Hall for a few weeks!' Daisy commented.

Revelations . . .

After a day or two in the States that's exactly what happened. America fascinated Martha, and she eagerly embraced every bit of the busy schedule Daisy had planned. At Phoenix Airport Daisy hired a car and they travelled through the red rocks of Sedona to the Grand Canyon.

'It's breathtaking!' Martha exclaimed as they took a plane ride over the sweeping grandeur of the Canyon. 'Look, a mule train winding down that narrow trail.'

Their next stop was Las Vegas. Daisy had been doubtful about its attraction for Martha, but Las Vegas was unique, a heaven for gamblers set down in the desert, and Martha Trevain wanted to sample the whole experience.

'Harry told me about this place. He had business meetings here, then he'd take his clients to the shows and the nightclubs. He never gambled himself, though — at least, that's what he told me.' She sighed. 'But there was so much he didn't share with me.'

'All this bustle and excitement! I know it's all glitz and glitter and there's heartbreak here, too: lost fortunes, gambling addiction, but — and you mustn't ever tell Jack — but I'm going to have a modest flutter.'

Daisy watched in amazement as Martha slid into a vacant seat at the roulette table and accepted a complimentary cocktail from a smiling waitress.

After half an hour Martha left the table.

'Well, done that, got the T-shirt. Not bad for a novice — I doubled my modest stake. I just want to see Caesar's Palace and the white tigers and then I'm done.'

'So, next stop California for a bit more sight-seeing, then a couple of days with Helen and Barrie Thompson,' Daisy said.

'I'm a bit apprehensive about that,' Martha confessed. 'Helen Thompson is very pleasant on the telephone and insistent that we go there, but she must know more about Harry than I ever did.'

'Don't worry, California will be fun.'

'It's just, well, California was Harry's home, too — a part of his life he kept completely hidden from me. What am I going to find there, Daisy?'

Whatever Martha's fears, she set them aside to enjoy the California experience. From Vegas they flew to Los Angeles and spent a couple of days enjoying the tourist spots so familiar from American films. Then Daisy hired a car to drive to San Diego on the spectacular coast road.

'Hmm, it's like Cornwall,' Martha said as they looked out at stunning beaches and craggy cliffs, 'only with better weather. This sunshine's heavenly!'

She enthused over San Diego, and its beaches with graceful pelicans wheeling over the cliffs and blue sea. Surfers, swimmers and sea lions shared the sea and the surf.

On their last evening before they met the Thompsons they dined out at their hotel California-style, outdoors on the hotel terrace, and watched a dramatic crimson-streaked sky as the sun sank slowly into the sea. Wonderfully tender juicy steaks, baked potatoes, the inevitable salads and fine red wine ended a wonderful holiday.

'It's been a fabulous trip, Daisy, thank you so much. I love England, of course, and Cornwall in particular, and I'll never leave it, but here in bright, scintillating California I can see how Harry was captivated, especially after war-torn England. Post-war England was pretty grim: rationing, austerity, cold winters.' She gestured towards the sea. 'Who wouldn't have preferred this golden land of plenty? The question is, why couldn't Harry share it with me and his Cornish family? He could easily have afforded it. A home in California, maybe here, with the boys . . . '

'Don't, Granny. We shall never really understand. Let's just enjoy our last evening here before we meet the Thompsons. Helen's sending a car for us tomorrow, and I'm taking mine back to the car hire firm.'

'That's kind. Shall we see Ben?'

'I think so. He texted me to say he would meet us at his aunt's.'

★   ★   ★

Barrie and Helen Thompson lived in a luxurious ranch-style house with a swimming pool in La Jolla, a smart coastal suburb a few miles from San Diego. Helen greeted them warmly and introduced them to her husband, Barrie.

'I'm sorry you haven't been well, Mr Thompson,' Daisy said.

He looked astonished. 'Me? I'm a fit as a flea. No problems.'

Daisy was puzzled. 'I'm sorry, I thought Ben said . . . '

'Oh, he got it wrong,' Helen said hurriedly. 'Would you like to sit by the pool, have a swim maybe, cold drinks, iced idea?' She spoke rapidly, moving nervously about the room.

'Maybe the folks would just like to sit quietly for a while,' Barrie said. 'They've had a busy trip, so I hear. Your first time in the States, Lady Trevain?'

'Martha, please. Yes, and I love it. I wish I'd come years ago.'

There was silence, more awkward than tranquil. Helen fussed about the seating area round the pool, moving chairs, adjusting the umbrellas.

The clear turquoise square of water looked so tempting that Daisy eyed it enviously. Everything was on such a large scale here, large houses, wide roads and streets, open spaces.

'Did my grandfather ever come here?' she asked suddenly.

Helen looked to her husband for help and he replied quickly, 'Why, no, we've only recently moved here.'

There was a pause before Helen said, 'Before, we were all — I mean, when Ben lived with us, he . . . Harry . . . did visit, when Ben was a baby, and later . . . they spent a lot of time together . . . ' She tailed off, then jumped nervously to her feet. 'I'll get us some lemonade, cool drinks . . . and I think I'll give Ben a call, see exactly what time he's coming.'

When she'd gone Barrie said, 'I'm sorry, Helen's jumpy today, not a bit like her usual self. You'll see why later. It's been so difficult, but right now let's all relax and get to know each other. Lady Trevain, how . . . ?'

'Oh, please — do call me Martha.'

'OK. So, Martha, tell us where you've been . . . '

Half an hour later Helen came back empty-handed.

'Lemonade?' her husband queried.

'Drat, I clean forgot. I've been trying to contact Ben. He'll be here shortly.'

Barrie looked at his watch. 'I'm sure

the sun's on its way down now, so Margaritas or cocktails? What do you think folks?'

'Sure.' Helen leapt to her feet again. 'Right away. Ahh . . . ' A car was crunching its way up the gravelled drive. 'That'll be Ben.'

She looked at her husband, an agonised expression on her face. He frowned, then nodded, as Ben appeared on the terrace.

'Hi, Martha. Hi, Daisy. It's good to see you both. How's the trip been?' Ben kissed them both on the cheek.

Daisy tried to ignore the impact on her senses of his appearance. In T-shirt and shorts, his skin tanned by the sun, he looked a very attractive model of health and fitness. She tried to avoid his eye but he was looking at her so intently it was hard to ignore him.

'You're looking well. America suits you, Daisy. Not missing Cornwall?'

She smiled. 'Of course, but there's so much to see . . . '

'I think now is definitely the cocktail

hour, Helen,' Barrie put in.

'They're ready in the sitting-room. Shall we stay out here, do you think, or indoors?'

Now even Barrie looked nervous. 'Maybe indoors would be more suitable.'

'What's the matter?' Ben looked from Barrie to Helen. 'You look more like you're having a wake than a welcome party.'

'I'm sorry, really I am,' Helen was near to tears, 'but it's got to be said. Your uncle and I, Ben, we've agonised so long . . . but we had to make a decision . . . '

'What? What on earth has happened? Is one of you ill?'

'Should we be here?' Daisy said. 'You look so serious. Is it a family matter? Perhaps Granny and I . . . ' She stood up but Helen gestured her to please sit.

'No. No, that's why you're here It *is* a family matter, a Trevain family matter . . . ' Helen said quickly.

'Shall I get the drinks?' Ben asked.

Helen looked at her husband, who shook his head. 'Best to get this over with first and then we'll go inside. We'll all probably need a drink.'

'For goodness' sake.' Ben frowned, 'what is it? You're scaring me.'

Helen closed her eyes for a few seconds then looked directly at her nephew.

'Ben, this will be a terrible shock, and please don't blame us — we were sworn to secrecy before your grand . . . before Sir Harry died . . . ' She stopped and gazed appealingly at her husband. 'I can't do it, Barrie, you tell him.'

'All right. Ben, there's no easy way to tell you this.' He cleared his throat, then said very quickly, 'You are not Harry Trevain's grandson.'

All her life Daisy was to remember that moment — the total shock, the total silence, then Ben's quick intake of breath before he looked directly at her and smiled, his dark eyes registering puzzlement followed by relief and joy.

'Not Harry's grandson? Then who am I?'

'I'm so sorry, Ben,' he went on. 'I've wanted to tell you ever since Sir Harry died, and since the legacy . . . we just didn't know what to do.'

Ben shook his head. 'I've suspected this ever since I went to Cornwall. After meeting the real Trevains . . . well, there's nothing of them in me. It felt . . . well, it felt wrong. So, who am I? Not even your great-nephew, Aunt Helen?'

'Oh, yes. You are my sister's grandson. My sister Ava Williams was your grandmother, but Sir Harry is not your grandfather, although in later years he came to believe he was because to him you were the ideal child, and lately the ideal man — so he . . . laid claim to you.'

'Perhaps we should go inside, dear,' Barrie said. 'Margarita or coffee — or iccd tea? To help cushion the shock.'

In the general movement Ben took

Daisy's hand and turned her towards him.

'I knew it,' he breathed. 'What I feel for you — it wasn't possible . . . We'll talk later.'

They followed the others to a spacious sitting-room with an ocean view framed in a huge picture window. It was here they heard Helen Thompson's sad story.

'I was seven years old when Harry Trevain came into our lives, working with the US War Department. The United States had just joined the war. My beautiful older sister, Ava, was nineteen years old, just out of high school, and she and Harry fell so in love. I'm sorry, Martha, this must be painful . . . '

'No, not any more. You see, Harry's letter explained . . . '

Helen nodded. 'That's something, at least.'

'Remember, I was a small child, so most of the drama went over my head — and I left home early to work in

Europe. But, of course, Ava's tragedy touched me constantly. She and Harry had a child, a baby boy who only lived a few days. Ava suffered terribly from post-natal depression and was almost suicidal when Harry returned to England.'

Martha said, 'Our first son was born in 1945 and Harry stayed in England for a year or so before going back to the States.'

'And from then on Harry was a tormented soul.' Helen drew a breath. 'Barrie, the drinks, on the side table, I think we need them.'

Barrie served ice-cold cocktails in silence.

'I won't say 'cheers',' Helen said, 'not until I've got this over.'

Her husband bent to kiss her. 'You're doing fine, dear,' he reassured her and she gave him a grateful look.

'Basically, the affair went on, until Harry made a break in the early Fifties — declared it over for good, and returned home to Cornwall where he continued to build his business empire.'

'But he did return to Ava?' Daisy said.

'Yes, because Ava wrote to him. She was in trouble. On the rebound from Harry, she had met a man — strangely enough a friend of Harry's from the same regiment. She became pregnant, and this time the baby boy lived, but the father was killed in a car accident. Once more Ava became deeply depressed, again suicidal, so I wrote to Harry. He came at once, and that was the beginning of his permanent double life. He was in love with both Martha and Ava, torn between the two families, unable to leave either totally.'

'What about Ava's baby?' Daisy asked.

'Harry took him on as a son, and gave him the Trevain name. That was Percy, Ben's father.'

'So I have no Trevain blood connection whatsoever?' Ben asked.

'None, except that Sir Harry, as the years went on, became convinced that you *were* his own flesh and blood. He loved you so much, Ben, he *wanted* you to be his grandson, and in his later years that's what you were.'

'And Ava . . . ?'

'Ava died soon after your parents were killed in Africa. And once they were gone we adopted you, and Harry continued to be your grandfather. He admired you so much, Ben.'

'Unlike his own boys,' Martha said sadly. 'I'm afraid he came almost to despise them. Daisy was his passion, the ideal granddaughter — as Ben was his ideal grandson.'

There was a long silence. The drinks remained untouched until Ben picked up his glass and raised it to his aunt.

'Aunt Helen, thank you. Thank you so much for everything. I'm so glad you could be honest at last.'

'I made a solemn promise to Harry that you would never know the truth until he was dead. Believe me, I had no idea about the huge legacy.'

'Which, of course, I can't accept

now,' Ben said firmly.

'But you must . . . ' Martha said fiercely. 'You must for Harry's sake.'

'But I'm not entitled!' Ben protested.

'But it's what he wanted,' Daisy insisted, 'and I can see now what he meant. My promise to him was to help you to help our family achieve harmony. You've made such a difference in Pencreek. Look at Christopher, my father . . . '

'There's still Peter Trevain.'

'We can deal with that,' Martha said firmly. 'Daisy's right, Harry knew what a shake-up it would be, leaving you his fortune. He meant it to happen, his last throw of the dice, to bring his own sons to their senses. You can't go back on it now.'

'We can set up a Trevain Foundation.' Daisy was quick to take up Martha's theme. 'Please, Ben, think about it.'

He looked at her for a long minute, then took her hand. 'Aunt Helen, would you excuse us, just for a few minutes? I have to speak to Daisy.'

'Not at all, dear, I shall enjoy talking to your aunt and uncle.' Helen was now beaming with relief.

'In here, Daisy.' Ben opened the door to a small study off the sittingroom. 'This is Aunt Helen's hideaway.'

'I don't need to think about this, Daisy. I need to tell you I've fallen in love with you. I knew you couldn't be 'family' because of what I feel for you ... and what I think you feel for me ... ' He took her in his arms and kissed her, at first tenderly, then with increasing passion.

Daisy, her heart singing with happiness and relief, kissed him back.

When they finally broke away Ben said, 'I reckon Sir Harry knew just what he was doing, sending me to Cornwall. It was to meet with his beloved granddaughter.'

'I'd like to think so. It all makes wonderful sense, Ben Trevain.'

They kissed again, free to express their passionate love, free to make plans to unite the Trevain family in the harmony Sir Harry had longed for.

'I love you, Daisy Trevain,' Ben said as he kissed her again, holding her close. 'You will marry me?'

'You know I will. I've always loved you — and there's so much we can do . . . '

'We'll worry about the future later. I've no doubt we'll have a legal battle on our hands about my inheritance! But for now . . . ' He kissed her passionately again and Daisy surrendered to the blissful present.

SUSPICIOUS HEART
EDEN IN PARADISE
SWEET CHALLENGE
FOREVER IN MY HEART
TWISTED TAPESTRIES
ALL TO LOSE

We do hope that you have enjoyed reading this large print book.

Did you know that all of our titles are available for purchase?

We publish a wide range of high quality large print books including:
Romances, Mysteries, Classics
General Fiction
Non Fiction and Westerns

Special interest titles available in large print are:
The Little Oxford Dictionary
Music Book, Song Book
Hymn Book, Service Book

Also available from us courtesy of Oxford University Press:
Young Readers' Dictionary
(large print edition)
Young Readers' Thesaurus
(large print edition)

For further information or a free brochure, please contact us at:
Ulverscroft Large Print Books Ltd.,
The Green, Bradgate Road, Anstey,
Leicester, LE7 7FU, England.
Tel: (00 44) **0116 236 4325**
Fax: (00 44) **0116 234 0205**

ELUSIVE LOVE

Karen Abbott

Amelia has always been determined to marry for love . . . but with her elder brother dead and posthumously branded as a traitor, Amelia and her sister find themselves penniless and ostracised by society. When a relative contrives to put an *'eligible parti'* under an obligation to make Amelia an offer, Amelia has to decide whether or not to stand by her principles . . . and face the consequences of turning down what might be her only chance to escape her unbearable situation.

MARRIED TO THE ENEMY

Sheila Holroyd

Faced with the choice of death or marriage to a stranger, Kate marries Lord Alvedon, the powerful servant of Queen Elizabeth. Taken away from everything she has ever known Kate finds it difficult to adjust to the strange new world of Elizabeth's court. Her innocence not only threatens her marriage, it puts her in great danger — and, unknown to her or her husband, a secret enemy plans to kill both of them . . .

TABITHA'S TRIALS

Valerie Holmes

Tabitha is reluctantly released from St Mary's Establishment for Impoverished Girls because Miss Grimley will not break the rules and allow her to remain. She must go into service, contributing to the school so that other girls will benefit. Tabitha rides on the back of a wagon and watches her past drift into the distance. With a heavy heart, she contemplates years of hard work and predictability stretching before her, little realising just what the future has to offer . . .